D0996201

Also by Dan Walker

SKY THIEVES
DESERT THIEVES

THE LIGHT HUNTERS

DAN WALKER

uclanpublishing

For Charlie, Maddie and Ivy

The Light Hunters is a uclanpublishing book

First published in Great Britain in 2020 by
uclanpublishing
University of Central Lancashire
Preston, PR1 2HE, UK

978-1-9129791-0-3

1 3 5 7 9 10 8 6 4 2

Set in 10/16pt Kingfisher by Becky Chilcott

A CIP catalogue record for this book is available from the British Library.

Printed and bound in Great Britain by Clays Ltd, Elcograf S.p.A.

"You ask me what Light is? Light is everything. Every single thing. The very fabric of our world is made up of this force – people, trees, the chair I am sitting on, this pen I am writing with. Few can access Light, control it. You are one."

Professor Majeson Medela

· CHAPTER 1 ·

"If there's one thing I am absolutely and utterly sure about," said Maya Murphy ducking under her desk on the classroom floor, "it's that Mr Winter is a monster."

"If anyone's a monster around here," said Lux Dowd, "it's you."

Maya checked her watch. "I mean, look at the time." She pushed the device up to Lux's face. "Does that not say five to three?"

"Yes."

"And what time do we finish school?"

"Three."

"And how long did the last Monster drill take?"

Lux thought back to the previous time their teacher had got them to overturn their desks and practise in case of a Monster attack. "Half an hour."

"Exactly."

For Lux, it had been a long day. Not only was Maya in one of her moods, but also their regular teacher, Mr Garside, had been off sick with a stomach bug. In his absence, Lux and his classmates had suffered through yet another day of grumpy Mr Winter. And now, just five minutes from the bell, when they'd all been about to go home, Mr Winter had announced a Monster drill. Even Lux had to admit, it was ice-cold.

"Now remember children," said Mr Winter crisply, standing with his hands on his hips, "what's the most important thing to do during a Monster drill?"

The kids replied as one. "Don't panic."

"Louder."

"Don't panic!"

Mr Winter walked up and down the line of tables. "I hope everyone's safely tucked away." He nudged a pair of boots at his feet, prompting a small girl to shuffle backwards. "These Monsters all have excellent eyes, you know? They can see a child from over a mile away."

Lux and Maya backed up against the wall. "Does he think we haven't done this before?" whispered Maya irritably.

She was right. Lux could recall twelve Monster drills that year, and more the previous. To most of his classmates, they were a complete waste of time. But Lux knew better. Indeed, the last time a Monster had crashed into town – a slavering, three-headed Cerberus as big as a house – Lux had lost both his parents and his sister. Even the Light Hunters had been unable to save them. Still, why their teachers considered it vital to practise a Monster drill *every* single month, Lux had no idea. *Especially not,* he thought, *at five to three on a Friday afternoon.*

Maya took a pair of metal compasses out of her back pocket and started to scratch absently at the table leg. "Are we still set for tonight?"

"Shh," said Lux, looking quickly at Mr Winter.

"Don't worry, he can't hear us."

"Yes, but someone else might."

Maya looked at the boy under the table with them, who was staring curiously at the rubber end of his pencil, as if it might turn into a cat. She gave Lux a have-I-made-my-point look. "Seriously, are we all set?"

"Yes," Lux sighed.

"I've nicked those black jumpers off the other girls at the orphanage. We should be able to sneak in. The library won't know what's hit it."

"We're not going to *hit* it," said Lux, frowning. "Look, Maya, if you can't take this seriously . . ."

Maya sat up straight. "I can. I can. I want to come. Especially if it's really there."

"I said I *think* it'll be there."

"That'll do."

"You'll have to be sensible," warned Lux.

Maya spread her arms, elbowing the boy with the pencil. "Sensible is my middle name."

Numpty, more like, thought Lux affectionately.

He caught his reflection in the classroom door window. His messy, mouse-blonde hair hung around his ears, and he had dark bags under his blue-green eyes. Lux had stayed up late the past few evenings, long after his grandpa and the old man's live-in carer, Miss Hart, had gone to bed, planning his and Maya's mission into the town library. This one was important. He had to get it right.

"Ahem."

Lux blinked. Mr Winter had returned from the other end of the classroom and was crouching in front of them.

"Yes, sir?"

"Lux Dowd, are you with us?"

"Yes, sir, I'm with you."

"Are you sure? Because for a minute there I thought you'd seen a Monster."

"Only you, sir."

Maya giggled. Fortunately, Mr Winter seemed to have missed Lux's joke. He looked at Maya with a confused expression, then back at Lux sternly.

"Have you two remembered it's a test next week?"

"We can't wait, sir," said Lux.

"Is that right?" Mr Winter held Lux's innocent gaze. Then he saw Maya's carving in the table leg. His brow furrowed. "Who did this?"

Lux and Maya didn't respond.

"I'll ask again, who did it?" Mr Winter pointed at the table leg.

Lux turned so he could see. Carved messily into the wood were two words and a symbol.

LIGHT HUNTERS <3

"Who was it?"

Lux looked at Maya, whose eyes were wide, panicked.

"Maya," said Mr Winter, "I've warned you three times today about your behaviour. This seems like just the kind of thing you'd do."

Maya said nothing.

"The headmistress takes graffiti very seriously. If she found out a student had been carving Light Hunters into one of her tables, she'd be extremely unhappy. If I was responsible, I'd own up now. Better a detention with me at the school play this evening than a visit to the head's office."

Lux looked again at Maya, who was rigid with fear. She'd been in trouble so often that year that the owner of her orphanage, Mrs Piper, had threatened to ground her if she got in trouble again. Lux took a deep breath.

"It was me, sir."

Mr Winter looked at Lux. "You?"

"Yes, sir."

"*You?*"

"Yes, sir."

Mr Winter studied the carving. "You've clearly been spending too much time with this one." He nodded at Maya. "I'd have expected it from her, but not you."

"Sorry, sir."

"Mmm . . ." Mr Winter chewed his lip absently as he considered what to do. "Well, seeing as it's a one-off, I'll let you off a detention. But if I see anything like this again, you'll be in big trouble. Is that clear?"

"Yes, sir. Sorry, sir."

"Get some sandpaper out of my desk drawer. You're not going anywhere until all that's gone."

Mr Winter fixed Lux with a final, disappointed stare and continued down the line of tables. Lux breathed a sigh of relief.

"Thank you," said Maya.

"You owe me," said Lux irritably. "Why did you *do* that, anyway?" He ran his fingertips over the carving in the table leg. "You know what people think about Light around here."

"I don't care," said Maya bluntly. "My friend's uncle says he knew one of the Light Hunters. He said they were never as bad as everyone says. I think the whole hating Light Hunters thing's baloney anyway. Maybe if we weren't so mean and horrible to them in this town, and we let them defend us, we wouldn't have to keep doing Monster drills every ten minutes. Speaking of which," Maya tapped her watch impatiently, "class ended ten minutes ago."

"Be happy you're not here all night."

Maya elbowed Lux in the ribs, but he didn't feel it. His attention was focussed on the words she'd carved into the table. He traced them in his mind, recalling everything he'd learned about the Light Hunters from the secret books he kept in his wardrobe, and he smiled.

· CHAPTER 2 ·

When Mr Winter finally let them go, Lux said a hurried goodbye to Maya and rushed back to the clock repair shop where he lived with his grandpa. Gathering up everything he'd need for their mission that evening, he scoffed a quick dinner of scrambled eggs on toast and raced to the harbour. He found a quiet spot away from the early evening strollers and spent the next hour rehearsing his plan, waiting for Maya. He spotted her balancing on a narrow wall by the promenade.

"Get down."

"All right," said Maya defensively, "you're as bad as Mr Winter." She hopped off the low wall and stood with her hands on her hips. "Before we start, I want to get one thing straight: are you honestly telling me – *honestly* – there's a Gauntlet in the lighthouse?"

"Yes." Lux crossed his fingers behind his back.

"A real Light Hunter one?"

"Yes."

"The magic-wielding, Monster-killing Light Hunters?"

"Yes!"

Maya eyed Lux as if he were having her on and shook her head in disbelief.

Lux knew there was no Gauntlet, but the lie was necessary. Maya's gullibility, and her love of gadgets and technology, meant that when Lux was deciding who to take with him on his mission, the answer had been obvious. Pretend there was a Light Hunter Gauntlet in the lighthouse – that most iconic of Hunter gadgets – and just like that he'd created an offer too good for Maya to turn down.

"I brought binoculars," she said helpfully, pulling them out of her bag.

"Nice one."

"And . . ." Maya reached into her leather satchel, "I also brought a compass and a lamp, and I've got this amazing . . ."

Lux tuned out. He was studying the moonlit tower through the binoculars. The lighthouse had been converted to a library nine years earlier. Had it still been a lighthouse, Lux would have found it duller than school on Maths day. But as a library, with its corkscrew of bookshelves, it contained something extremely important. And after two long weeks of planning, Lux was finally about to lay his hands on it.

The lighthouse stood at the end of a rocky pier on the outskirts of town. The moon cast a silver glow that brought to mind creepy stories Lux's grandpa had told him. Between the tower and their position on the promenade was the harbour, jammed with boats and fishing nets. It smelled of seaweed and salt. Every so often, the silence was broken by a loud *plop* as one of the townspeople walking the pier looped a stone into the water.

Maya handed Lux a black jumper and started to wriggle into her own. "Do we really have to swim?"

"No," said Lux, "we can just walk down the pier."

"Really?"

"Definitely. Then someone will see you and go tell Mrs Piper you're not really performing in the school play, and that you're actually about to break into the lighthouse with Lux Dowd. She'd love that."

"I suppose not," said Maya thoughtfully.

"I've told you, this little outing needs to stay secret. If anyone sees us we'll be in big trouble."

"But I get the Gauntlet, yes?"

Lux clasped his belt and strapped on a pair of swimming goggles. "Yes, you get the Gauntlet."

Down the promenade, five large, stone statues commemorated the handful of Monster attacks that Lux's hometown, Daven, had suffered over the past century. Every town had a similar memorial. Closest to Lux was the multi-headed Cerberus that had smashed Daven when Lux was two, killing his family and half the town's residents. Lux climbed so he was standing on one of the statue's three heads and traced a path across the busy harbour to a narrow staircase that led to the pier. From there, they would approach the lighthouse, smash the first-floor window and slip inside.

"Are you absolutely sure it's going to be there?" asked Maya dubiously.

"The Gauntlet?"

"Your book."

"I hope so."

"What if it's not?"

Lux shot Maya a fiery glance. He jumped down to the water, took off his socks and dipped a foot. So cold. He almost pulled it straight out again, but thoughts of his ill grandpa forced him to keep it under. He dunked his other foot quickly, then his legs and finally his head. He resurfaced, teeth chattering.

"Well," he said to Maya, "are you coming?"

· CHAPTER 3 ·

Maya's question reminded Lux of an evening six months before, when his grandpa had first informed Lux he was dying. Lux didn't know whether the antique book in the library would contain what he needed to cure his grandpa, but he wasn't just going to sit there like everyone else, hoping for a miracle. Lux had already lost his parents and sister. He wasn't going to lose his grandpa too.

Maya slid silently into the water behind him and together they swam between the boats. The silvery moonlight was bright enough to see the ships' names, Lux's favourite being a scruffy fishing trawler called *'Fraid Knot.' I must remember to tell grandpa that one when I get back,* he thought.

They cleared the tangled mess of crafts and emerged into the harbour. The promenade lay a hundred metres behind now, the lighthouse an equal distance ahead. Lux had spent many summers with his grandpa swimming in lakes around Daven. Maya, despite promising that afternoon she'd beat him in a race to the lighthouse, was not a strong swimmer. Lux stopped to get his bearings and noticed she was a good distance behind, kicking and splashing noisily as she fought to keep afloat.

"Shh!" he said, looking anxiously at the people on the pier.

"I can't," cried Maya. "I'm carrying all the stuff."

She had a point. Lux swam back to take some of the weight. He allowed her to lean on him and catch her breath.

"How much longer?" she asked.

"Five minutes," said Lux. "Maybe ten."

"Ten!" Maya exclaimed. On the pier, a couple walking hand in hand looked in their direction.

"Five," whispered Lux. "Definitely five."

The water in the middle of the harbour was much colder than near the promenade. Lux's fingers and toes had all gone numb, and he swam faster to warm them. How had he forgotten it would be this cold? The previous winter, a boy at Lux's school had gotten into trouble falling through ice on the canal. Lux intended to avoid such a fate. He pushed Maya away and motioned for them to continue.

Now they were approaching the lighthouse, Lux had a decent view of it for the first time. He went over the plan again in his head – how they'd climb the pier steps without being seen and locate the best window to get inside. In his hurry to get to the harbour from his grandpa's workshop, Lux had forgotten to bring a hammer. *Oh well,* he thought, *I guess that's what rocks are for.*

The book Lux was searching for he'd learned about after writing to Professor Medela, expert in Light-healing at faraway Lindhelm University. Lux had requested the professor's help with his grandpa's illness and had received a brief reply two weeks later:

Dear Lux,

Whilst I admire your tenacity, I really must inform you that there is nothing I can do for your grandpa. I am unsure if you know this, but everything in our world is made up of Light – people, the chair I am sitting on, this pen I am writing with. And yet, in spite of its ubiquity, our comprehension of Light is such that we are not even close to understanding it well enough to cure a long-term illness – despite what so-called experts in Light-healing might have you believe.

I hope you find something to help you soon. Whatever you do, I must ask that you refrain from contacting me again. Twelve letters are plenty.

Sincerely,
Professor Majeson Medela.

P.S. If you must persist in your search, try looking up a book called Investigations into Light and Healing by the former Light Hunter Amanda Sedgewick. Amanda has come closest to unravelling your particular puzzle, even if her secrets will not solve it.

Lux had rushed to the lighthouse the next day to take out the book but had struggled to find it on the overstuffed shelves and

Mrs Henderton, the grumpy, eagle-eyed librarian, had scowled at him when he'd asked. Refusing to give up, Lux had narrowed the book down to a locked chamber at the top of the lighthouse where Mrs Henderton kept an ever-expanding collection of objectionable books. Those about the Light Hunters, and particularly Lux's book about Light-healing, certainly fit into that category.

Lux had travelled three-quarters of the way to the lighthouse when he realised he'd heard nothing of Maya for a while. Happy she'd finally worked out how to swim quietly, he turned to give her a thumbs up.

But Maya was gone.

Lux peered into the darkness. Where was she? He took off his goggles and wheeled around, searching. Panic wrenched his stomach, and he swam quickly back to where he'd last seen her. He listened for her breathing. Nothing. He whispered her name – at first quietly, and then more urgently. "Maya. Maya!"

A thousand thoughts assaulted Lux all at once. Had she gone back? Or had she swum ahead? Had she been thrown off course? Or had she . . . drowned? He winced at this last horrible notion, feeling suddenly guilty for lying to her.

No sooner had this thought entered his mind than it was knocked forcefully aside by another, this one significantly more frightening. Just ahead, poking out of the water, was a large shark fin. Lux floated, both paralysed and amused at the same time. The very idea of a shark as far north as cold, wintry Daven made him laugh, despite his racing pulse. Only when the fin rose, revealing the glistening torso, spiked head and razor-sharp teeth of a large creature, did Lux realise he wasn't looking at a shark at all. It was something much, much worse.

It was a Monster.

· CHAPTER 4 ·

Lux froze. He knew, like every little kid who'd trembled through scary bedtime stories, that there were Monsters in the oceans. Indeed, the land outside towns and villages was full of them. They'd been around thousands of years. Some even attacked human settlements – like the three-headed Cerberus that had killed Lux's family. But these were the biggest of the big. The creature in front of Lux was no town-destroyer. In fact, it seemed to be Monster spawn – a smaller Monster hatched from the mother. All the same, Lux knew he was in grave danger. *Why did I do this?* he asked himself crossly, forgetting his grandpa's illness in the heat of his fear. *Why? Why? Why?*

The Monster had spotted Lux and was studying him closely, its slit eyes flicking back and forth. It tilted its spiked head, holding Lux's wide-eyed gaze, and then rushed forwards. Lux flinched. He tasted panic and fear like metal in his mouth. Every inch of him wanted to swim away, but he couldn't. Maya was his best friend. She had been as long as he could remember. He had to at least *try* to rescue her.

Lux spun his goggles rapidly around his wrist and tossed them to his right. The Monster heard the *splash* and jerked its head, swimming towards the spray. Taking a breath, Lux dived underwater. Briefly, he saw the fuzzy outline of the Monster powering towards the goggles. Then it was gone.

Now where?

Lux pulled himself through the swell, searching for Maya. The harbour water was murky, but the moonlight was just strong enough to make out dull shapes below the surface. He studied them like a hunter, growing more and more worried by the second. His lungs were burning, but he swam on. Most of the shapes were too big or small to be Maya, but he kicked towards them just to be sure. He shook them and pushed them away, realising they were all just clumps of seaweed.

Lux's vision began to grey. He kicked to the surface, sucking in cool air as he searched for the Monster. Bubbles broke the surface. Once more, an urge to escape swept through Lux, but thoughts of Maya stopped him. *One more look,* he promised himself. He took a breath and submerged.

Lux waved his hands in all directions, desperate to find his friend. He swam into something heavy and his heart jumped with excitement. But when he wrapped his arms around it, he realised it was just a sack of potatoes.

It was then that he felt a firm tug on his arm.

Lux turned, ready to lash out. But instead of the Monster, he saw his friend. He dragged Maya towards him, motioning for them to rise. Together, they kicked up and broke the surface, where they coughed and sucked in salty air. Lux noticed a pained expression on Maya's face.

"There's a Monster," he said.

"I know," she said shakily. "It bit my leg."

Lux shifted her in the water to get a look at the wound. Just then, there was a bubbling sound behind her and a ferocious growl as the Monster surfaced. The creature's jaws yawned, revealing rows and rows of jagged teeth. Without making a sound, Lux mouthed a single, panicked word.

"Swim!"

· CHAPTER 5 ·

Lux spun rapidly so he was facing the beach beneath the promenade and chopped at the water, trying to put as much distance between him and the Monster as possible. He'd made it only a few metres when he realised Maya wasn't following. Looking back at her round, frightened eyes, he understood immediately. She couldn't move. Swimming back, Lux hooked an elbow under Maya's armpit and dragged her away. The Monster rocketed after them.

Panic ripped through Lux. He dragged Maya as fast as he could, hacking at the water with his free arm. On his back, he could see the Monster dashing towards them, closing in. Lux kicked out at the creature's head, but he missed and connected with its neck.

"Damn!"

The Monster was on them, thrashing with razor claws, which

tore into Lux's thigh. He groaned as he tried to wedge himself between Maya and the Monster. Lux bunched his fists and swung at its head. His punches barely seemed to touch it, and after a while, the Monster moved to attack Lux's exposed back. The pause allowed Lux to send in one last fist – a ferocious strike that rammed into the Monster's eye with a sickening *squelch*. Lux corkscrewed his wrist, driving it in further.

The Monster reared in pain and sank under the waves. Grabbing Maya, Lux pushed harder even than before, pounding the water with his hands. He groaned when the beast resurfaced, black liquid oozing out of its injured eye. The Monster located them, snorted a hot discharge and swam forward.

Lux and Maya were approaching safety now. Adults had gathered on the beach and were peering anxiously into the dark, trying to work out what was happening. *Don't just stand there,* thought Lux, *help!* At last, one of the men spotted them and waved them towards him. Lux adjusted his course. The Monster sped up, eating into their lead with long, easy swipes. Sickness welled up again inside Lux. The pain in his thigh and his burning lungs made him want to quit. How could he possibly beat a Monster?

A loud clap rang out.

A gunshot.

The Monster reared, emitting a deep, guttural roar, pain etched across its face, webbed arm clutching its chest. It collapsed forward. Lux watched it bob about and cheered inwardly as it sank beneath the waves.

And then he was amongst a blaze of hands, first prising him

and Maya apart and then lifting them out of the water. A man stood in the shallows with a gun, looking vigilantly down the sight. Lux watched him until he was lowered onto a dune. The sand felt good against his skin. He sucked in air as the adults surrounded him. A large lady with kind eyes forced them back and knelt by Lux, cradling his face. Lux squirmed out from under her and staggered upright.

"Where's Maya?"

His question was met by a confused look. He barged past the woman. *Where is she?* Lux's muscles burned fiercely, but he managed to keep his footing. He found Maya on another dune and dropped down by her side. She looked even worse under the streetlamps than she had in the water, so that Lux had to stop himself crying. Her body was riddled with slashes.

But it wasn't these that made Lux want to sob.

It wasn't the cuts that tied a knot in his throat.

It was the injury to Maya's leg.

· CHAPTER 6 ·

Lux was no stranger to cuts and bruises. He'd often hurt himself jumping between the rotting groynes on the beach after school. And he could remember adventurers being carried through Daven marketplace on stretchers after running into Monster spawn on their way back from nearby Kofi, or whilst returning from the ancient ruins that littered the region. But he'd never, *ever* encountered an injury as bad as Maya's. How would she ever forgive him?

Lux peeled back the fabric of her drenched trousers. Her leg was a mess. Her shin had dislocated at the knee and gashes climbed her calves, turning the skin an angry, swollen purple.

Lux supressed a shudder. A few adults gasped and walked away. Lux appealed to those remaining for help, but nobody seemed to know what to do.

"Help her!" he cried desperately.

Lux collapsed onto the sand. An idea entered his mind, something he shouldn't have been thinking. *Not now,* he thought, *not here.*

The large lady who'd helped Lux earlier knelt by Maya and laid a hand on her forehead. A second lady joined her, taking Maya's hand. "Has anyone gone for an ambulance?"

"It won't get here in time," said the first lady. She slid a bamboo stick out of her hair, lifted Maya's bad leg and tore the trouser fabric. Maya moaned softly and settled. "She's lost a lot of blood." The lady directed her next question at Lux. "What were you *doing* out there?"

Lux ignored her.

"What can we do?" said a young man in the crowd.

The lady glared at him as she stroked Maya's hair. "It'll be all right," she said soothingly.

Lux had heard those four little words before, the first time he'd marched into Daven hospital to see what could be done about his grandpa's illness. He knew what they meant: nothing. The thought sent a shiver up and down his spine. Surely someone could help? Surely one of them could do *something*?

It was then Lux's forbidden thought returned, something he'd promised his grandpa he'd hide from the town. And yet, seeing Maya – so hurt, all because of him – it was impossible to ignore. How could he stand by doing nothing when he might be able to help her? Surely his grandpa would understand.

Before Lux could stop himself, he was standing between

Maya and the crowd. He ignored the confusion on their faces and positioned himself next to Maya's injured leg. Taking two deep breaths, he brought his hands in front of his chest and joined each thumb and forefinger. An electric shock zipped from his core to the top of his head and down his arms, making them vibrate. A fuzzy-edged, blue-white Light orb formed between Lux's fingertips, growing brighter by the second. The orb crackled, generating thin wisps of Light. It felt like starlight was rippling through Lux's fingers. The orb grew until it was as big as his head. Then he clapped. A flash lit up the beach and the orb shot towards Maya, its plasma exterior breaking on her skin. She cried out as it exploded in another Light shower, this one excruciatingly bright. Everyone on the beach covered their eyes, holding their arms up in the fierce onslaught. Then the Light disappeared.

One-by-one, all the adults lowered their arms and blinked. Lux had collapsed at their feet, shivering and shaking. The adults regarded him and Maya. What they saw left them speechless.

Maya's leg was completely healed.

· CHAPTER 7 ·

Lux avoided their gazes, tracing patterns in the sand with his finger. A young man knelt beside Maya and ran a gentle hand along her shin, shaking his head in disbelief.

"Did he just . . .?"

"Yes," said the large lady furiously, "and he shouldn't have." She glared angrily at Lux, before draping her coat over Maya. "Stop gawping and get some blankets," she barked at her husband.

Lux screwed his fist into the sand. What had they expected? Maya was badly hurt. Was he just going to sit there twiddling his thumbs? Yes, he knew throwing Light was banned in Daven. It had been since the Cerberus attack. Other towns might rely on the Light Hunters to keep them safe, but not Daven. Not anymore.

Lux's grandpa had drilled this into him, even as he'd secretly taught Lux the ways of Light in his workshop basement.

"You may have a talent," his grandpa told him repeatedly, "but you must never, *ever* show anybody what you learn."

Until that evening, Lux had kept his promise. He'd needed little encouragement. The last person caught throwing Light in Daven had been banished. Yet, this punishment had failed to stop Lux practising in secret. He trained daily, always fascinated by what he could do with his hands. Early on, his grandpa had identified in Lux a talent for healing – rarest of the three Light arts. Lux had learned the basic casts, trained them until he could heal better than he could fix clocks. But always in secret, always away from those who would see another Monster attack ahead of a dabbler in Light.

But now he'd let his secret slip.

All he'd wanted was the lousy book. Was it really that hard? Why hadn't the stupid librarian just given it to him? If she had, he could have found out whether it contained the cast he needed to heal his grandpa and none of this need have happened.

But Mrs Henderton had done the opposite, leaving Lux with no choice but to steal it and injuring Maya in the process. A pang of guilt struck Lux. And yet . . . another part of him was angry. Furious, even. Why should he feel guilty? Were it not for him, Maya's leg would still be wrecked. Why should it matter if he'd thrown Light? What right did everyone have to tell him off?

Lux got up, fists bunched. "Why shouldn't I?"

The large lady eyed him sharply. "Excuse me?"

"Why shouldn't I use Light?"

"You know why."

"No, I know everyone *says* I shouldn't throw Light. I know everyone round here's scared of it. But I don't know *why*. Isn't she healed?" Maya was sitting up now, colour returning to her cheeks. "Didn't I heal her?" He looked at the adults. "Grandpa always told me to hide this. Keep it secret. And what's come of that? Nothing! My grandpa's still dying and there's nothing any of you can do to save him. At least I'm trying."

The young man who'd spoken earlier shuffled forward to comfort Lux, but the lady stopped him. "I think you should go home," she said.

Lux opened his mouth to argue but changed his mind. What was the use? Without another word, he pressed his forehead gently to Maya's in goodbye and walked up the beach.

The crowd had thickened somewhat since they'd been rescued, with more onlookers making their way over to see what was happening. Lux quickened his pace and started towards the promenade. A part of him wanted to throw another cast to spite the lady – perhaps *Protect* – something bigger than the *Heal* he'd used to fix Maya. *How'd you like that?* he thought. But something made him stop.

A man was leaning against the lamppost at the bottom of the stairs. He was broad, with a craggy, pocked face, thick ashy hair and trimmed white beard. His hands were stuffed into the pockets of a scruffy leather overcoat, covered with black belts and straps. A pair of boots and a dark, wide-brimmed hat completed his outfit.

But it was the man's eyes that stopped Lux in his tracks, staring with a fierce intensity. They reminded him of a predator's eyes – cold, lifeless. Lux felt suddenly hot and looked away, almost disoriented. When he looked again, the man nodded, tipped his hat slowly and walked up the stairs into the shadows.

· CHAPTER 8 ·

Lux checked to see if anyone else had seen, but they all seemed preoccupied with Maya. Something about the stranger had spooked Lux. Who was he? And why had he been staring? Lux hung back a full minute before making his way up the stairs. On the promenade, he remained under street-lamps, hurrying between pools of yellow light and checking nobody was following.

The route back to his grandpa's workshop was long and winding, taking him along the promenade that contained Daven's trinket shops, through the beautiful memorial gardens built to commemorate those lost to Monster attacks, between the old, decommissioned Light-tram lines and through a series of narrow alleys and little side-streets. On the way, Lux passed a procession of his favourite shops – some he visited with Maya, others with his grandpa. His favourite was a sweet shop called '*Mrs Miggin's Sugar Rush*,' with its kaleidoscope of multicoloured jars twinkling brightly in the window. Lux had tried every sweet at one point or other, and he longed for a bag now.

"There's not a grumpy face in Daven that can survive a bag of Mrs Miggin's sweets," his grandpa was fond of saying.

Lux clenched his jaw tightly. The entire purpose of the evening had been to get hold of Amanda Sedgewick's ancient Light book. If it contained what his grandpa needed, as Professor Medela had suggested, there was a chance Lux might cure him. While Lux was a good Healer, his knowledge of Light was limited to what his grandpa had taught him. The *Heal* he'd used on Maya, *Protect*, *Catch*, and *Remedy* were all good casts, but they weren't powerful enough to fix his grandpa. For that, Lux needed the book. Not only had he failed to steal it, he'd broken the only promise his grandpa had ever asked of him.

Lux felt rotten.

His grandpa's shop was located off Daven's main square – a cobbled space that housed bakeries, butchers, banks and taverns. It consisted of a crumbling, two-storey building, painted royal blue and decorated with gold lettering that read '*Dowd & Grandson.*' Lux was proud his name was on the sign. He cleaned it every week so that it gleamed next to the buildings nearby.

The large clock that hung on the square's north tower read eight thirty-six. Lux's curfew was eight. If his actions at the beach hadn't been bad enough, now he'd get it from his grandpa and Miss Hart for being late. The thought made Lux want to carry on walking. But it was raining, and he was feeling hungry. And that man at the beach . . .

Lux hurried down an alley and into the shop's back garden, where he slid his key into the door. Removing his coat, he stood still, listening for his grandpa or Miss Hart. Nothing. What were the chances? How many times had he been caught coming in late? Too many. Lux smiled at his good fortune. Rubbing his growling belly, he tiptoed towards the kitchen.

The room was dark, lit by a wedge of moonlight falling through a crack in the blinds. Lux picked out the curved edge of a dinner plate – mashed potatoes, vegetables and chicken. Although it was almost certainly cold, it smelled amazing and his stomach somersaulted at the sight. He turned on the kitchen light, but instantly his heart sank. Sitting at the table, doing little to hide her irritation, was Miss Hart.

"And just where, might I ask," she demanded, pulling up a second chair, "have you been?"

· CHAPTER 9 ·

Miss Hart had moved in a week after Lux's grandpa informed him of his illness. She arrived unannounced, with a single black suitcase and a sealed note for the old man. Lux's grandpa had read the note, rolled his eyes, thrown it into the fire and shown Miss Hart to the spare room.

Where had she come from? Why had she suddenly turned up? Lux had no idea. He'd been desperate to find out, but the chance to ask had never arisen. In the end, he'd grown so accustomed to Miss Hart being around – making his grandpa's bed, tidying his room, washing his clothes and reading him books in the evening – that the question no longer seemed important.

She was in her late teens, with sleek, black hair tied neatly in a plait. She had a kind, oval face, with arresting, bright blue eyes. During the week, she wore black trousers and a black shirt. If she was going out, black shoes, black coat and scarf. Only at the weekends did she allow herself a little colour, and then only a mauve scarf to replace the black.

Miss Hart was confident beyond her years – bold enough, in fact, within her first week, to order Lux's grandpa back to bed when he tried to do the dishes after a long day in the shop. She was protective of her role and demanded things be done according to her precise wishes. So that when Lux tried to help by ironing his school clothes on the last day of summer holiday, Miss Hart had rolled her eyes pityingly at his feeble attempt and ironed them all again.

"I've seen screwed-up paper smoother than this."

Despite her reprimands, Lux had grown to like Miss Hart, who was like the big sister he'd never had. Miss Hart, for her part, had taken a shine to Lux too.

She had her limits though and late nights were one.

"Well?" she said huffily, her arms folded. "Where've you been?"

Lux tried rapidly to come up with an excuse but failed. What could he possibly say that she'd believe?

"You were looking for that book again, weren't you?" Miss Hart had found out about Lux's search when she'd discovered one of the letters he'd written to Professor Medella stuffed behind his bed.

Lux screwed his heels into the kitchen floor.

Miss Hart sighed wearily. "I've *told* you, Lux, if you keep bugging Mrs Henderton, your granddad will find out sooner or later and get upset. You don't want that, do you?"

Lux shook his head. Of course he didn't want that. The movement highlighted a smear of blood on his neck. Miss Hart grabbed him for a closer look. She noticed his ripped, damp clothes.

"What have you been doing?"

Something about the concern in Miss Hart's voice made lying impossible for Lux. "I was going for the book."

Miss Hart looked at him. "Did a *shark* have it?"

"No." Lux pulled back. "Well . . ." He pictured the Monster, ". . . kind of. It's still in the library. Mrs Henderton wouldn't let me have it, so I . . ." he paused, ". . . I thought I'd break in and steal it."

"You what?" Miss Hart's voice shot up.

"I had no choice," said Lux defensively. "I have to heal him."

Miss Hart shook her head. She'd spent the previous week trying to convince Lux that there was no single secret in any book that would heal his grandpa.

"But why are you so wet? And your neck?"

Lux stuffed his hands into his pockets. "We didn't want to get caught, so we swam across the harbour."

"We?"

"Me and Maya."

"You got Maya in trouble too?" Miss Hart's eyes popped open.

Lux grimaced. "When we were in the water, Maya got bitten. It was a Monster."

Miss Hart waited for Lux to crack a smile. When he didn't, she leaned in. "A Monster?"

"It was just spawn," said Lux quickly. "I think. It definitely wasn't a normal animal."

"How badly was she bitten?"

"She's . . ." Lux scratched his chin. Miss Hart didn't know about his ability to throw Light. How could he put it without giving anything away? "She's okay now," he said carefully. "It hurt her pretty bad."

Miss Hart took a clean cloth, ran it under warm water and dabbed Lux's neck gently. "Did you tell anybody?"

"There were adults there when we got Maya out of the water. Someone shot it."

Miss Hart cleaned Lux's neck in silence, thinking. She gripped his shoulders and held him at arm's length, eyeing him shrewdly. "Are you having me on about this?"

"No, and I still didn't get the book."

"Oh, book shmook," said Miss Hart dismissively. "I think you're *very* lucky to be alive Lux Dowd. Not many people survive Monster attacks, even spawn. You're *not* to do anything like this again, do you understand?"

Lux nodded.

"And don't go telling your grandpa about it either. He's got enough to worry about without you piling it on."

Miss Hart paced the kitchen floor. "A Monster." She shook her head, astonished. "Listen, your grandpa wants a word with you. He's been waiting. I suggest you eat your dinner, then go through. In the meantime, I'll get you some clean clothes." She walked to the door as Lux scooped up a heaped forkful of mashed potato. "And remember," said Miss Hart, wagging a warning finger, "not a word."

· CHAPTER 10 ·

Once Lux had eaten, he changed into his pyjamas and slipped through the short corridor that connected the shop with the back of the house. He couldn't for the life of him think what his grandpa might want unless it was just to tell him off for being out late?

His grandpa's bedroom was small and had seemed even smaller since the onset of his illness, when he'd shifted his coffee table, books, reading lamp and newspapers through to keep him company. Aside from the hours he worked in the shop, he spent most of his time in his bedroom, reading in his rocking chair or lying in bed and cracking jokes with Lux.

The room was like those Lux had read about in his grandpa's old books, with polished wooden furniture and artwork-covered walls. Two framed certificates, naming Lux's grandpa Clockmaker of the Year, hung by his bed, next to a faded picture of Lux as a baby.

His grandpa removed a pair of glasses as Lux entered. "Finished saving the world for the evening?" he said as Lux leaned in for a hug.

"Naturally," said Lux, sinking into the sofa.

"Two dragons or three this time?" His grandpa stroked a long, grey beard.

"Three tonight. They nearly ate the lighthouse!"

"Did they?" The old man raised an eyebrow.

Lux fidgeted in his seat. His grandpa was kidding around, but it was clear that deep down he was annoyed. Lux twisted a loose thread on the sofa.

"Am I right in thinking Miss Hart's already told you off for being late?"

"Yes," said Lux.

"Good. Because that's the fifth time in as many weeks. It must stop, Lux."

"I know."

"We worry about you," said his grandpa, stuffing a large pillow behind his back. "Where've you been anyway?"

Lux thought back to what Miss Hart had said about not upsetting his grandpa. He wanted to lie, but if his grandpa had yet to hear about Lux's evening at the beach, it would only be a matter of time. It would hurt him less to tell him now.

So that's what Lux did. When he'd finished, his grandpa stared. "You're certain it was Monster spawn?"

Lux recalled the slobbering beast – its cold eyes and terrible stench. "I think so."

His grandpa stroked his beard again. "That's not good – not good at all. There hasn't been a Monster sighting this close to Daven in a long while. It wasn't good you throwing that cast either. That'll come back to haunt us. I'll be surprised if we don't have people knocking on the door first thing tomorrow."

"Sorry," said Lux glumly.

"Pah!" His grandpa waved away the apology. "The girl was at death's door. Nothing to be sorry about. Still, could have done without it." Lux's grandpa ground his teeth, his brain working like an engine. His concentration seemed to fade and he smiled, a twinkle in his eye. "Did it work?"

"What?"

"The cast? *Heal*?"

"Perfectly," said Lux. "Totally healed."

"Well done." Lux's grandpa patted his shoulder. "Told you you're getting better. You'll be fixing me next."

Lux frowned. In truth, he was a long way from fixing his grandpa.

The bedroom door clicked open and Miss Hart entered carrying a tray of food. She made room for it on the bedside table, looking across quizzically at Lux and his grandpa, aware of the silence.

Lux tucked his knees to his chin on the sofa. "Miss Hart said you wanted to speak to me."

Lux's grandpa accepted a steaming cup of tea from Miss Hart and took a sip. "I did, but I think it's a bit late now. You could have done with knowing before you went out."

"Knowing what?"

Lux's grandpa placed the tea on the table. "It was more of a warning."

"There's been a stranger hanging around town," Miss Hart cut in abruptly. "He's been watching children, asking after them."

"What does he look like?" asked Lux. But before either Miss Hart or his grandpa could answer, a terrible, creeping sensation overcame him. The man at the beach? The one in the hat? An image of the stranger sprung to Lux's mind. He listened carefully as his grandpa described him perfectly, feeling shakier with every word. Lux looked at them, his discomfort clear. Lux's grandpa raised himself up on his bed.

"Lux, it's nothing to worry about . . ."

"I saw him," said Lux. "I've seen him."

· CHAPTER 11 ·

Miss Hart, who was topping up his grandpa's tea, spilled a little on the carpet. She bent instinctively to clean it, but Lux noticed that, as she did, Miss Hart inclined her head ever so slightly and exchanged a meaningful glance with his grandpa. No words were spoken, but a strange tension warped both their faces. Then it was gone. *What's it about?* Lux wondered. There was something they weren't telling him.

Lux's grandpa ruffled his newspaper. "Hmm," he said pensively. "Where was this man?"

"At the beach."

Miss Hart stood up and speared Lux with a glare. "You told him?"

"Of course he did," said Lux's grandpa. "Carry on, Lux."

"He was standing by the promenade," said Lux, trying to remember. "He was looking at me."

"At you?"

"When he saw I'd seen him he walked off." Lux paused, hesitant. "You don't think he was looking for *me*, do you?"

"No no," said his grandpa quickly. "I'm sure he was just surprised by your little show." He ruffled the newspaper again. "As was everyone, I expect!"

Lux frowned. There was definitely something they weren't telling him. A moment's silence passed in which Miss Hart fussed about the room – drawing curtains, tidying away books, picking up clothes. Lux's grandpa watched her, smiling reassuringly when he caught Lux staring. He slapped a bony knee.

"Well," he said, "I think you've had enough fun for one night, young man. Time for bed."

Lux moved to protest, but the firm look in his grandpa's eyes told him he wouldn't get very far.

"We'll see what comes of all this in the morning," his grandpa went on. "Speaking of which, I think you should stay around here tomorrow. Just to be on the safe side."

"But . . ."

"No buts."

Lux bit his tongue. He gently butted his forehead to his grandpa's – their way of saying goodnight since Lux was little.

"I'm sorry," he said. "About all of it. I was just trying to help."

"I know," said his grandpa, smiling patiently. He tilted his head, gesturing for Lux to go to bed. Lux said goodnight to Miss

Hart. When he reached the door, his grandpa called to him. "Lux?"

"Yes?"

"If you see that man again you stay away from him, all right?"

Lux nodded.

"Night, pal."

Lux closed the door and waited in the hall as Miss Hart moved busily around the room. He heard her muffled voice through the wood. Something about the look she and his grandpa had shared worried him. What were they hiding? Was there something he should know? Lux tiptoed to the door, careful to avoid a creaky wooden floorboard. Their voices were clearer, but he still couldn't tell what they were saying. Nevertheless, Lux heard the same tension in their voices as he'd seen in their faces. He listened a while longer, before deciding it was no use and giving up.

Lux's bedroom was located at the back of the house. He'd chosen it for its view, which gave him a direct look at the ocean. At night, Lux would watch storms pummel the water, their purple and grey lightning forks lashing out just like Light casts. He'd view such storms differently now after his evening with the Monster. What else might be lurking beneath the waves?

Apart from a bedside table, wardrobe and desk, there was little in Lux's room beside a single bed. He took the only photograph he had of his family and kissed it once. This ritual complete, he delved into his wardrobe and brought out a wooden chest that had once belonged to his sister. It contained a small library of books, mostly about the Light Hunters. One was a leather notebook, which according to Lux's grandpa had been given to his sister during a visit to her school by Artello Nova, the Light Hunters' Luminary.

The Hunters, until shortly after the Cerberus attack, had been the world's foremost Monster fighting force. They still were in most places, but in Daven and Kofi they'd fallen into obscurity – accused of failing to stop the Cerberus attack. A Light-ban had quickly followed.

To Lux and Maya, however, the Light Hunters were heroes – masters of Light, good, brave people who risked their lives every day. Saving villages, towns and cities was all in a day's work. Even though Daven had turned on the Hunters, Lux and Maya still loved them. Even though the Hunters had failed to save their families, Lux and Maya still wanted to *be* Light Hunters. And that little leather notebook – the only remaining link between Lux and his older sister – had stolen his heart.

According to his grandpa, Artello Nova had instructed Lux's sister and her classmates to sketch any Monsters they encountered in the book. Lux had always wanted to add something of his own. Now, finally, he was able to.

He spent a while sketching the Monster at the harbour, trying to capture its sharp teeth and spikes. When he finished, he returned the book and chest to his wardrobe and slipped into bed.

Even though Lux was in a good mood, it took him a little while to drift off to sleep that night. In the dark, an image whirled around his mind, one that jerked him awake with feelings of panic.

That man by the beach . . . who was he?

· CHAPTER 12 ·

Lux woke early the next morning. He lay in bed, listening to birds tweeting outside his window, trying to work out if anyone else in the house was awake. After a while, he figured the way was clear. Getting changed, he swiped an apple from the kitchen and crept out into the chilly morning sun. He felt a little guilty about ignoring his grandpa's warning. And he was worried about what might happen once word spread around Daven that he'd used Light. But he had no intention of sticking around to speak to the police – certainly not when his only crime had been healing his best friend. No, Lux had a busy day planned. And it started with an apology.

Maya lived just down the street from Lux in the orphanage that had been built for the children who'd lost their parents in the Cerberus attack. Lux dashed there now, dropping into *Mrs Miggin's Sugar Rush* on the way to buy a bag of toffee pieces – Maya's favourite. He arrived at the orphanage's front door and knocked twice. Mrs Piper answered. When she saw it was Lux, she scowled and slammed the door in his face.

"News travels fast," he muttered.

Lux hurried to a nearby alley and clambered over a wooden fence into the orphanage's garden. He tossed a sweet at Maya's window. The toffee bounced off the glass and splashed noisily into a pond, leaving a brown smear where it had hit the glass. Maya's frowning face appeared.

"Mrs Piper says I'm not to speak to you," she announced coldly.

"I know," said Lux. "I just wanted to say I'm sorry."

Maya disappeared. Lux tapped his foot impatiently, waiting for her to return.

"Maya!" he hissed. "Talk to me. Please."

Lux listened for a response, hoping she'd change her mind. He *had* healed her, hadn't he? Or did that count for nothing? After a minute, he sighed in defeat. He turned to go but was stopped by a sharp whistle. A hand appeared in Maya's window, beckoning him up. Lux grinned. Stuffing the bag of toffees into his belt, he pulled himself quickly up the drainpipe, swung open her window and spilled inside.

Over the years, Lux had probably spent as much time in Maya's bedroom as he had his own. It was messy, with an unmade bed, dirty plates and half-empty cups on every surface. Posters lined the walls and piles of unwashed clothes sat in every corner. There were rubber bands, pencils, screwdrivers, scissors, lengths of wire and so many gadgets on the floor that Maya could have set up her own market stall.

She had been fascinated with technology as long as Lux could remember. It was an obsession that came at the expense of school, meaning that Maya never achieved the grades her teachers thought she could. ("Why do *they* care anyway?" she'd often ask grumpily.) It had also earned her a reputation as a bit of an odd-bod. But Lux knew that what Maya lacked in grades and popularity, she more than made up for in technical skill. What Maya couldn't do with a screwdriver and rubber band wasn't worth doing.

Lux brushed off his trousers. "Hi."

"Hello," said Maya awkwardly.

"I uh..." Lux pulled at a loose thread on his shirt as he searched for the right words. He unhooked the crushed bag of toffees from his belt and handed them to Maya. "I got you these."

Maya took the sweets and sat on her bed. "Why didn't you tell me?"

"Tell you what?"

"You know."

"The Gauntlet?"

Maya's flinty stare told Lux she wasn't in the mood for jokes. "Your Light!"

"I wasn't allowed," said Lux glumly. "Grandpa told me not to tell anyone." *And besides,* he thought, *what was I supposed to say? That I can do the one thing in this town nobody's allowed to do . . .*

"But you could have told *me,*" said Maya.

Lux bit his lip.

"You healed me," she added, brightening up. "I can't believe you can actually manipulate Light. You're like a Light Hunter!"

Lux grinned. Maya had never been able to stay angry at him for long. And just like that she was back to normal. A hundred questions spilled out of her. Could Lux believe they'd been attacked by a Monster? Where did he learn to throw Light? What casts could he do? Was he *sure* he wasn't a Light Hunter? Who taught him? Did Light hurt? Could he use it to get out of homework?

Lux answered as many questions as he could. But after a while a glance at his watch told him he'd better get moving. He threw up his hands, begging Maya for mercy.

"Stop!" he said, lowering his voice quickly to avoid alerting Mrs Piper. "Please. I've got to go."

"And *I've* still got questions to ask!" countered Maya doggedly, scoffing another toffee.

"Seriously," said Lux. "Although . . ." an idea suddenly occurred to him, "you can come with me if you want."

Maya stopped chewing, a shrewd look on her face. "You're going to meet some Light Hunters, aren't you?"

Lux laughed. "I'm going to the hospital. You should come."

Maya sighed. "I can't."

"Come on," Lux coaxed.

"I honestly can't." Maya pointed to a gadget-themed calendar on her wall. In the box for that day's date was the word 'sister.'

"Oh. That's today?"

"Yep." Maya grimaced. "Another weekend with my elder sister.

I'll be spending the day packing, and then tonight I'm getting a bus."

"Can't you pack later?"

Maya swept a toffee-covered hand over her room. "I don't even know where my underpants are. It's going to take me a whole day just to find stuff."

"You're sure?" checked Lux.

"Sure, sure," said Maya reluctantly.

In which case . . ." Lux got up off the bed, ". . . I'd better get going."

Maya unlatched her window. For a moment, their eyes met. "Next time," she said seriously, "tell me what's going on, yeah? We're supposed to be friends."

"I will."

From inside the orphanage came the sound of a slamming door. Maya froze, listening for footsteps outside her room. Satisfied the coast was clear, she took the bag of Mrs Miggin's toffees Lux had given her and poured some into his hand.

"Now, get out of here Light boy, before we get caught."

· CHAPTER 13 ·

Climbing down the drainpipe with a handful of sticky toffees turned out to be a lot harder than Lux anticipated. But somehow he made it without alerting Mrs Piper or any of the other orphans. Lux felt better now he'd apologised to Maya. She'd been desperate to join him on the mission to the lighthouse, but ultimately he was responsible for her injury. He was glad she'd forgiven him.

Clambering back over the fence, Lux landed heavily in the alley. Stuffing a sweet into his mouth, he pulled a small piece of scrap paper and a pencil out of his pocket. The to-do-list, put together that morning while he was waiting in the queue at Mrs Miggin's, contained four items. He drew a line through the first.

1. ~~Apologise to Maya.~~
2. Visit the hospital.
3. Try the lighthouse again.
4. Do homework (no!)

Daven hospital had recently relocated outside town, to a building that had once belonged to the local Light Hunter squad. Lux liked the hospital's new home, as the only way to get there was to catch a tram. With his nose pressed up against the window, Lux would stare wide-eyed as the wooden and stone buildings of town changed slowly to rocky, verdant coastal road. The journey took half an hour – much slower than the old Light-trams, according to his grandpa, who'd moan about it whenever he had the chance.

It was late morning by the time Lux arrived. He took his usual, circuitous route through the wards – greeting long-term patients and telling them silly jokes ("what do you call an alligator in a vest? An investigator.") – before taking a lift to the doctors' offices. As usual, they rolled their eyes irritably at his appearance.

"No," they answered, when he enquired if they had any new ideas about how to cure his grandpa. "The same no as last week, and the week before, and the week before that."

Lux had never understood why they got so grumpy with him. After all, there was no harm in asking.

After a quick lunch in the food hall – jacket potatoes and cheese, one of Lux's favourites – he visited the hospital library, where he read about his grandpa's illness, trying to find anything that might help. As usual, he came away disappointed.

It was late by the time he finished. Lux thought of his grandpa and Miss Hart, and how much trouble he'd be in when he finally got home. A part of him wanted to stay at the hospital and avoid the headache. But he knew he'd have to face them sooner or later. Better to get it over with.

The evening sun was setting by the time Lux got the last tram back to town. The car was almost empty. He selected a seat at the back, leaned against the window and dozed. Half an hour later when he woke, his fellow passengers had all alighted, and he found himself alone with the driver. Outside, the coastal road had morphed back to the stone and wood buildings of town. Lux judged they were about five minutes from the station. He spent this time chatting to the tram driver about her day. When they finally pulled in, he thanked her and jumped down.

"Be careful," warned the driver, shutting off the engine. "I've heard word there's a stranger hanging around, watching kids."

In the day's rush, Lux had forgotten all about the man in the hat. He shivered.

Lux's grandpa had always described Daven as a spiderweb, with roads radiating off a central square. Lux hurried down one now – Murgaton Drive – heading inwards. During the tram ride, a leaden, gloomy sky had descended, and it was raining – big, heavy, drops that thudded off the concrete. Lux had meant to take his grandpa's umbrella that morning, but in the hurry to get to Maya's orphanage he'd forgotten. Instead, he lifted his canvas bag above his head. A couple of men scurried down the now-empty street.

Lux's clothes were soon drenched, and he huddled briefly in a doorway, tipping the collected water from his bag before walking on. A little further along, a broken-down cart blocked the road. Beside it, looking just as damp and miserable as Lux, was an auburn-haired young woman of about Miss Hart's age. Lux walked on for a few paces, then looked at her again. Her make-up was oozing down her face and her eyes were close to tears. He couldn't just leave her. He walked over.

The lady's cart was a half-wooden, half-metal vehicle with a Light-motor attached to the rear. Such vehicles were prohibited since the Light-ban. What was she doing with one? Lux wondered. He could tell the motor was broken as it spat thin blue sparks of Light, and he could smell burning. As he approached, the woman's face brightened. Lux quickened his pace, avoiding puddles in the road. But when he got close, the entire scene changed. An intense white Light bloomed at the front of the cart. The woman stamped her boot and stepped smartly to her left, assuming a position at the head of three other black coat wearing strangers – all of whom had been hidden behind the cart. They saluted someone off to their right.

"Lux Dowd, isn't it?" called a voice from the shadows. Lux searched but couldn't locate its owner.

"Y-Yes," he said uneasily, looking again at the four who'd saluted. What was going on?

"I'm keen to speak to you. You have something that interests me."

Lux flushed. "Are . . . are you the..?"

The gentleman laughed. "I believe some in your town have called me the man in the hat." His voice was sonorous, quiet. "Though I go by other names. You can call me Deimos." The man's rough hand slid out of the shadows. The four people in overcoats lowered their salutes, spun smartly on their heels and entered the cart. The last inside shut the door as Deimos stepped forward. He inspected Lux, his wrinkled, coarse hand lingering. He looked just like he had before, with black overcoat, black trousers and boots. And yet, in the cart's Light, he seemed older. His hair, which had appeared silver in the moonlight, carried a tinge of blonde. His clothes were patched, sewn where they'd been torn. He was a big man, with a bulbous nose and scrutinous, squinting eyes.

"I saw your little performance at the beach." As Deimos spoke, he inched towards Lux, joining his hands so that a burst of red energy expanded between them. "Quite remarkable for one so young. The rumours about you are true."

"What rumours?" Lux looked to see if there was anyone else on the street, but it was empty.

"You know what I'm talking about."

"That I can throw Light?"

Deimos smiled humourlessly. "Many can throw Light, Lux, whether they know it or not. Few can do what you did last night. None without special training."

The man's odd voice – loud one moment, quiet the next – and his position between Lux and the pavement, made Lux feel nervous. He tried to continue home but Deimos blocked his path.

"I-I want to go," said Lux shakily.

"A boy with your powers should use them. My . . ." Deimos paused, choosing the correct word, ". . . organisation could help you in this task."

Lux squinted. "What organisation?"

"We're . . . engineers." Deimos casually flicked a wrist, sending out a spark of red energy towards the cart's Light motor, which twisted and unravelled until it was like new. There was a blaze of Light and the motor rumbled to life. "We're trying to engineer a new world – a world where people need not be afraid."

"I'm not afraid," lied Lux.

"You *should* be." Deimos's eyes flashed wildly. "Even your grandpa doesn't truly understand the power in you. Only I can teach you to harness it. Together, we can make the world a safer place."

Deimos's mention of Lux's grandpa threw Lux. How did Deimos know his grandpa? And what was he talking about? Safer place? It didn't make sense. What *did* make sense was that Deimos, and the people in the cart, made Lux want to run as far away as possible.

Again, Lux tried to push past, but this time Deimos flicked his right hand and threw a *Wall* cast to block Lux's path, its pulsing red energy fizzing in the rain. Lux's grandpa had shown Lux *Wall* casts and how to pass through them. Lux tried now, but when his boot hit the barrier, he was thrown violently backwards. He tried again, but again the *Wall* shunted him. A crawling, prickling panic climbed Lux's legs. He shouted at Deimos.

"Let me go!"

"Difficult, Lux. Someone with your talent is . . . precious." As Deimos said the words, the cart door opened, revealing harsh orange light and the grim faces of the four inside. Deimos signalled for Lux to enter.

"I-I have to get home," said Lux feebly, fighting to steady his voice. He looked around for help. Where had all the other people on the street gone?

"I'm afraid I can't allow that."

Lux's heart thudded in his chest. All the blood had drained from his head and he was struggling to focus. What could he do? The *Wall* still stood over his right shoulder, the immense bulk of Deimos ahead, and to his left was the cart. Lux looked at the houses and shops, which seemed to lean menacingly inwards. He felt like shouting for help, but his throat was dry. A single tear ran down his cheek.

"All I want," said Deimos coolly, "is for you to show me what you can do."

"How about I show you what *I* can do instead?"

The voice had come from Lux's right. Deimos looked around at the same time as Lux, an irritated snarl curling his lips. Squatting on the greengrocer's roof across the road was Miss Hart. Only this was no Miss Hart Lux had seen before. Gone were her black clothes, replaced by a thick grey jacket, cut off at the shoulders, and olive shorts. Her hair was no longer tied in a neat plait, but rather spiked and frizzed like a wild cat. A mauve sash swept back from her shoulder and a dark mechanical contraption wrapped around her left forearm.

Miss Hart motioned for Lux to approach. Lux backed away from Deimos, who flicked a wrist to dismiss his *Wall*. Simultaneously, the cart door slammed shut, plunging the street into darkness. Deimos stepped forward, his entire demeanour changed.

"I'm sorry," he said pleasantly, "are you lost?"

"If anyone's lost around here, I'd say it was you," said Miss Hart.

A mask of intense rage disfigured Deimos's face. He leapt without warning at Lux, crossing the ground between them at terrifying speed. Suddenly, a blue arc of Light appeared at Lux's feet. The Light traced a line up to the roof behind him, forming a loop around his ankles. *Hang on a minute . . .* But before Lux could finish his thought, he was jerked rapidly upwards so that he hung like a fish on a line. He made a faint "hmphh" as the Light whipped him up and over the edge of the roof, depositing him next to Miss Hart. Lux looked at his feet. The Light there faded, retracting into the device around Miss Hart's wrist.

"What's going on . . .?"

Miss Hart silenced Lux with a warning glare.

Deimos stood in the road, unsure what to do. A burst of raucous laughter down the street announced a group of young men spilling out of the *Dog and Bell* pub. Deimos tilted his head in their direction and then back at Miss Hart and Lux. But they were already gone, scudding along the greengrocer's roof. As Miss Hart gripped Lux's wrist, he turned to watch Deimos, who arrowed back to his cart, signalling orders at his deputies. The last Lux saw of him was an electrically-charged shower as he hurled a furious, frenzied *Bolt* at the waterlogged ground.

· CHAPTER 14 ·

Miss Hart didn't speak to Lux on their way back to his grandpa's workshop. Lux tried to slow his breathing as he battled a heavy, sinking, sick feeling in his stomach. When Miss Hart stopped to examine the skyline and check they were still heading in the right direction, Lux studied the contraption on her wrist. It was made of a dark metal, and intricately carved with delicate, gold swirling patterns. Wisps of pale-blue Light fizzed at its edges, tattooing the metal. Lux couldn't help but think it resembled the Light Hunter Gauntlets he'd seen in his sister's books. But surely it couldn't be? How would Miss Hart have got hold of one of those?

They came to a sloped roof overlooking the town square. Once Miss Hart was satisfied they'd lost Deimos, she picked out Lux's grandpa's shop. Arriving at the roof, she pulled open a wooden hatch and gestured for him to climb inside.

"What's happening?" Lux asked. "And what's that thing on your wrist?"

"Later, Lux. Just get inside."

A serious, focussed look on Miss Hart's face convinced Lux not to argue. He slid through the hatch and made his way down a ladder into darkness.

"I didn't even know this existed," he said, swiping a cobweb off his cheek.

Miss Hart closed the hatch behind her. It smelled strange – old and dusty. Miss Hart gripped Lux's wrist and felt up and down the wall. She found a latch and pulled. A warm glow spilled in as a door swung open, highlighting antique grandfather clocks and boxes of spare parts. Lux noticed some of the clocks were the old Light-powered sort.

"Miss Hart, please tell me what's going on."

"We have to see your grandpa."

She led him downstairs to the living quarters, where they found Lux's grandpa standing in his bedroom doorway, worry clouding his face.

"Thank goodness you're safe," he said breathlessly, embracing Lux.

"Of course he is," said Miss Hart.

She slid past Lux into his grandpa's room. Lux and his grandpa followed. "You shouldn't have snuck out this morning," he said, depositing Lux on the sofa. "What did I tell you about sneaking out?" Before Lux could answer, his grandpa turned to Miss Hart. "Was it him?"

Miss Hart pulled back the curtains and peeked out of the window. She nodded. "A minute later and . . ."

Lux stood up, agitated. What was going on? How did his grandpa know about the man?

"Be careful," said his grandpa, "you need to rest."

"*You* need to rest," Lux replied, realising suddenly that his grandpa was up and about. "You should be in bed."

"Not tonight."

"We really don't have time for this," said Miss Hart, picking up a rucksack and stuffing it with Lux's clothes. "We have to get out of here."

Lux looked between Miss Hart and his grandpa. "That man," he said to his grandpa, "the one you told me about . . . he spoke to me. He knows . . ." Lux hesitated. Could he tell Miss Hart about his Light? He decided he had no choice. ". . . he knows what I can do with Light."

Lux's grandpa exchanged a meaningful glance with Miss Hart. "Give me ten minutes."

"Five, and then we go." Miss Hart squashed everything into the bag and zipped it shut. She crossed the room with a confidence Lux had never known in her, like she was a totally different person. Was she really his grandpa's carer? Miss Hart shut the door behind her, leaving Lux and his grandpa in silence.

"Grandpa?"

The old man sighed heavily. He sat on his bed and took Lux's hand.

"Lux . . . things are about to change for you in a way I never intended. You must leave here tonight with Miss Hart. There's . . . someone after you. His name's Deimos." Lux's grandpa's face soured. "I knew him once, but he's no longer the man I knew. You have something he wants, and he won't stop until he has it."

"But why me? What is it I have?"

"You're special, Lux. You've never questioned how I've been able to teach you the ways of Light, but the truth is I've taught many people. None of them had your talent. You are more skilled with Light than most twice your age. You have a gift, one that hasn't even fully awoken yet. It's important this is not shared with Deimos."

"What do you mean?" said Lux shakily. How was he special? What gift? What skill. "I don't want to be special. I want to stay here."

"I know, but that choice has been taken from us. You must go with Miss Hart."

"Grandpa . . ." Lux hesitated, ". . . Miss Hart used Light. Who is she?"

"Her name's Ester. She's a Light Hunter – a Tech, to be precise. She can't *throw* Light like you can, but she's the best they have with a Gauntlet."

"That thing on her arm?"

"Yes, but none of this matters right now. All you have to know is that you can trust Ester. You need to go with her tonight."

As if she'd been listening outside the door, Miss Hart re-entered. She dropped Lux's rucksack at his feet.

"That'll have to do," she said. "If we don't go now, he'll find us."

Lux's grandpa looked directly into Lux's eyes. "Don't be afraid," he said. "Deimos is a dangerous man, but Ester will keep you safe. She's going to take you to the Light Hunters HQ – a place called Dawnstar. You'll be hidden there. You need to do exactly what she says."

Lux tried to focus, but his vision was spinning. He'd only ever been away from his grandpa once, when the old man had gone on a weekend fishing trip and Lux had spent a sweet-fuelled two days at the orphanage with Maya. The thought of their being apart had made him a touch anxious then; it terrified him now. And what about school? Or Maya? Or his grandpa's illness?

"I don't want to leave you," said Lux miserably. "I promised to make you better."

"We have to go." Ester nudged the rucksack at Lux's feet.

"You have to leave me," echoed Lux's grandpa, forcing a smile. "I'll be fine."

Lux frowned.

Ester knelt in front of him. "Lux, if we don't get out of here, you aren't going to be saving anyone. Deimos and his people will get here and they'll take you. That cannot happen. If you come now, we can save you. We're the best in the world at throwing Light. If anyone, anywhere can figure out a way to heal your grandpa, it's us. But you must come."

Ester hooked the bulky rucksack over Lux's shoulders. "She's right," said his grandpa, tightening the straps and helping him up. "You go there, find out what you need to fix me and come back. All right?"

Lux peered at him through bleary eyes. His voice was quiet. "Okay."

Ester jumped up and tapped the metal contraption on her wrist, projecting a flat, blue Light-image into the air. She studied it and swept it back into the machine.

"We have to go out the window."

Ester slid open the glass and dropped noiselessly into the back garden. Lux's grandpa nudged him gently after her. Lux sat on the smooth window-ledge, with Ester below. It had stopped raining now and the air was cool. Off in the distance, a ship blew its horn.

"Goodbye," said Lux's grandpa.

"Goodbye," said Lux.

And he dropped out of the window into Ester's arms.

· CHAPTER 15 ·

Ester lowered Lux to the ground, then pressed a little button on her Gauntlet. The Light-image appeared again. *Is it a map?* Lux wondered. Ester studied the image closely and shook her arm to make it disappear.

"We have to get to the skybus station," she whispered urgently. "We'll head through the back streets. Keep close."

Ester opened the gate. She checked their way was clear, then took Lux's hand and headed into the passage.

Daven's skybus station was a massive, towering, sandstone construction that loomed over town. Shaped like a honeycomb, each hexagon was a landing bay. In the air around it, skyships flitted like fireflies, jostling for an opening. Beyond, were the town's dual Monster watchtowers – the people inside alert to signs of a Monster attack.

The town-square alleys criss-crossed, serving the nearby houses. All the lamps that lined the passages were the old, deactivated Light-powered ones, meaning that as Ester and Lux moved they had to blindly avoid the detritus of town – dustbins, old Light-bicycles, broken tables and chairs. Lux bumped his knee more than once, letting out yelps of pain. While she waited for him to recover, Ester checked their location on her Gauntlet, glancing anxiously behind her.

At one point, she spotted two white cones of Light bobbing left and right down the alley. Quickly extinguishing her map, she yanked Lux behind an overturned bin and shoved a hand over his mouth to keep him quiet. They crouched in silence, their breathing shallow. After a minute, the figures drifted off down another alley and the Lights vanished. Though he was relieved, Lux couldn't help but think they'd find his grandpa. How could the old man possibly be okay?

"Will they go for grandpa?" he asked.

"They might," said Ester. "But trust me, he'll be fine."

Lux wasn't so sure.

A little warmer after their brush with danger, Lux was better able to keep up with Ester as she hurried along. He was amazed she'd managed to fool him. Kind, friendly, caring Miss Hart, a Light Hunter? A fighter of Monsters? A wielder of Light? It was unbelievable. Lux marvelled at this as they passed the buildings he called home – *Mrs Miggin's Sugar Rush*, his favourite musical instrument shop with the self-playing pianos, the abandoned factory in which he and Maya played hide and seek. Something about the abrupt way they were leaving made Lux think they wouldn't be coming back.

The skybus station had grown so large now that it towered over them. To their right were Lux's school playing fields, and the overgrown canal that backed onto his and Maya's classroom. High above, the day's final skybuses circled, their engines thundering loudly. As Ester drove them forwards down the alley, Lux realised they were headed for a dead-end. He tugged her jacket to tell her, but she barely seemed to notice. They reached the gate – a gothic, spiked barrier that the school caretaker locked at the end of every day.

"Damn!" said Ester when she tried to open it.

"I was trying to tell you," said Lux.

Ester paced down the alley as Lux tried the gate. No joy. Just as he was about to suggest an alternative route over the canal, he caught sight of two more Light cones down the alley. He nudged Ester.

"They're coming this way," she whispered. "I'm going to have to do something now. Something you've never seen. Whatever I do, don't say a word."

Ester sneaked down the alley towards the Light cones. She tapped the tool on her arm and a dim Light issued from within. It expanded swiftly until it touched the wooden fences either side of them.

"It's an invisibility shield," she explained. "It'll only last a minute. We've got to be quick."

Ester approached the school gate, working at her Gauntlet

again. This time, it produced a pale-blue Light-blade, which she tested on the wooden fence. It hissed softly as it cut through. Satisfied, Ester turned the blade on the iron gate and set to work, laying the discarded bars quietly on the path.

Behind her, Lux looked through the invisibility barrier at Deimos's people. One was the crying cart woman he'd seen earlier; her colleague was another of those in black overcoats. They approached the shield and shined their Light cones directly at it. Knelt on the ground, Lux felt his heart pounding furiously – *boom, boom, boom*. It was hard to believe they couldn't see him. He could smell their breaths. The pair squinted into the distance as if the alley ran for another hundred metres. Then the woman lowered her Light and together they hurried back the way they'd come.

Lux breathed a sigh of relief.

This Light Hunter stuff was really something.

· CHAPTER 16 ·

Ester had cut a hole in the gate large enough for her and Lux to squeeze through. *I've got to get hold of one of these Gauntlets*, Lux thought. They entered the school grounds, where Ester motioned for Lux to keep low. When they reached the street, Daven Skyship Station was just to their left. The road was busy, with people hurrying past on either side. Lux located the clock that hung on the skyship station wall. Seven forty-seven. He'd jumped off the tram back from the hospital at quarter to seven. Had it really only been an hour?

They had thirteen minutes before the last skybuses of the evening departed. After checking that no more of Deimos's people were nearby, Ester stepped confidently into the road.

The station's entrance was a huge, rounded arch, sheltering a wide run of steps. At the top was an enormous orange board that listed the evening's skybus destinations. Ester read it intently and marched towards the nearest ticket office. A young girl there had her nose buried in a paperback book.

"Can I help?" she asked, laying it aside.

"I'd like two tickets to Lindhelm," said Ester politely.

"Two shailings please."

Ester plucked two copper coins from her jacket pocket and handed them over. As she extended her arm, the girl noticed Ester's Gauntlet – dark chrome, tattooed with blue Light – and raised an eyebrow. Ester quickly retracted her arm. Lux shifted nervously, looking at the people still arriving in the atrium. He'd never been to Lindhelm. He had no idea what it would be like. The girl finished the transaction in silence, glancing at Lux every now and then. She slid the tickets warily to Ester.

"Platform 6F. Skybus should be there now."

A dozen staircases provided access to the upper levels, glittering black against the honeycomb of the rest of the station. Lux and Ester found the one leading to platform 6, which was much steeper than the stairway up from the street and wound in a tight corkscrew around the east corner of the building. Lux did his best to keep up as they climbed, but after a few levels he had to take a break, bending over to catch his breath. Was Ester forgetting he wasn't a Light Hunter?

Platform 6F was an enormous rectangular hangar with two platforms, between which hovered a waiting skybus. It smelled strongly of oil and smoke, and the far end of the hall was open to town, so that Lux felt an ice-cold wind freezing the air. The Monster watchtowers were visible through the opening, and beyond those a square section of inky blue sky, studded with stars.

Lux followed Ester towards the skybus, rubbing his arms to keep warm. To their right, the craft hummed as it hovered in the gap. It was a long double-decker, painted red and gold with green piped edges. Balconies jutted out front and back – one for each deck – and small staircases linked the balconies on either floor, spilling into the cabins which sported two rows of seats, either side of a plush, carpeted aisle.

Lux had travelled on skybuses before. With Monsters roaming the land, skybuses were the safest form of transport. This was especially true for Lux's weekend trips with his grandpa, visiting Kofi's famous zoo, or the town's twin waterfalls, or ancient Wutan ruins down the coast. But these had been mere jaunts. A flight to Lindhelm was something else entirely – a four-hour, uninterrupted slog over the fire trees of the Shengan Jungle. Maya would have been as excited as a mouse with a wedge of cheese. Lux, too, had he not been on the run from Deimos.

But he was.

And a hundred questions were stampeding through his mind.

Ester had found a quiet corner by a closed food stall where they could wait for the pilot to finish preparing for his flight. Lux joined her there.

"Ester," he said guardedly, "are you sure we can leave grandpa here? And who *is* Deimos? What does he want me to do?"

Ester glared at Lux, cautioning him to lower his voice. "Deimos is a dangerous man," she said quietly. "A very dangerous man."

"But *who* is he? Where did he come from?"

"It's best you don't know that right now. You're frightened enough."

"I'm not frightened," lied Lux.

Ester regarded him over the tip of her nose. "You should be. Your grandpa was."

"Grandpa wasn't scared."

"He was worried enough to contact us."

Lux blinked. Had he just heard that right? His grandpa had contacted the Light Hunters? How? When? And why hadn't he told Lux?

There was a long, heavy silence as he thought over what Ester had said. It was broken by the conductor's whistle, inviting passengers to board the skybus.

"Anyone for the eight o' clock to Lindhelm! Anyone for the eight o' clock to Lindhelm!"

Lux eased himself up ready to go, but Ester held him back. They allowed the remaining passengers to board, as well as the conductor, who hopped on the skybus and signalled for the pilot to take off. The engine rumbled noisily and a blast of steam erupted from its chimney. Ester leapt up and dragged Lux towards the rear viewing balcony. She hurled him off the platform and onto the bus. With each passing second, the craft floated further and further away. By the time Lux had righted himself, the gap had grown to two metres. His stomach shot to his throat. What if Ester was abandoning him? Would she do that? After she'd got him all the way there? His worries evaporated instantly when she raced towards the edge and leapt like a cat – soaring swiftly over the drop and landing perfectly on the bus.

Lux blinked. "You have *got* to show me how to do that."

Ester smiled knowingly. "Where you're going, Lux, you're going to learn much better things than that."

· CHAPTER 17 ·

There were only a few empty seats remaining when Lux and Ester entered the skybus cabin. Normally, when Lux travelled with his grandpa, he would race to the upper deck to get the best view. But he figured Ester was unlikely to be in the mood for this and instead shimmied into the window seat of the last row. Ester joined him, nudging him along and plonking herself down. She met his eyes briefly and squeezed his hand.

The Lindhelm skybus was significantly more luxurious than any Lux had travelled in, with green, velvet, padded seats and lots of space for him to stretch his legs. Hanging from the ceiling were little standing ropes with metal hoops, and a set of stairs climbed to the upper deck. Beyond, was the pilot's cockpit. Lux spotted him through the glass, happily humming a tune.

There were twelve people in the cabin, as far as Lux could see. None wore black overcoats. Ester looked over her shoulder at the ticket inspector, and then at the other travellers, who were cheerfully chatting away. She fidgeted.

"Is everything all right?" asked Lux.

Ester didn't answer.

"We are okay, aren't we? We just left him. He can't catch us now."

Ester checked the other passengers weren't listening. "I'm not sure you quite understand the man you're dealing with, Lux. Deimos won't give up. We might have avoided him in Daven, but he has people all over. Until we get to Dawnstar, *anyone* could be one of them."

Ester held Lux's gaze to emphasise her point. Lux didn't want to admit it but she seemed afraid. Suddenly, he felt a little ashamed. Ester had been sent to rescue him. *He* was the reason she was in danger, and all because they thought he was special. But they were all wrong. He wasn't special. Yes, he could throw a *Heal* cast. But contrary to what Deimos and his grandpa thought, he was no genius.

And what of all the other towns that needed a Light Hunter? What if somewhere was being attacked right now? Lux knew more than most the acute pain of a Monster attack. Ester should have been out there with her fellow Light Hunters, saving towns, not cooking dinner and washing Lux's school uniform. And what of Artello Nova? Lux recalled his sister's book collection, and all the pictures of the Light Hunter Luminary inside. Why was he so keen to protect Lux and how did he know Lux's grandpa?

The skybus banked sharply left, pressing Lux into the window. The jolt reminded him of just how long it had been since he'd been to the toilet. Close to bursting, he rose in his seat and slipped past Ester.

"Lux, you'd be better staying close to me."

"I need the toilet."

Ester looked anxiously about the cabin. "Be quick then."

The conductor – a tall, thin man with a pencil-moustache – was approaching from the balcony area when Lux made it to the rear passage. He pointed to a mechanical ticket machine around his neck. Lux shrugged as if to say he had no money and gestured to Ester.

The toilets were located next to the balcony exit. Lux nipped inside. When he re-emerged, the passage was still empty. After all that had happened, he was desperate for some quiet. Instead of returning to Ester and the warm cabin, he opened a window and leaned out of the skybus. Immediately, he was hit by a cold gust of wind.

Below was Daven. Lux tried to pick out any buildings he recognised. The lighthouse was obvious, as were the Monster watchtowers. Also recognisable was the skybus station, with its galaxy of skyships. More difficult to locate was the town square, although Lux eventually spotted the illuminated North Tower clock. From there, he was able to trace a line back to his grandpa's shop, which seemed as tiny as a toy model.

Deimos was somewhere down there.

The thought made Lux shiver.

He pushed himself wearily off the ledge and closed the window, ready to return to the main cabin. When he turned, he was amazed to see Maya Murphy standing in front of him.

"Lux?"

"Maya?"

"What are you doing here?"

"What are *you* doing here?"

"I'm going to see my sister. I told you this morning."

Lux thought back to his conversation with Maya at the orphanage. Had she said that? It all seemed so long ago. "She lives in Lindhelm?"

"You know she does. I can't believe you're here. Where are you going?"

Lux didn't know what to say. "I'm ... uh ..."

Maya hopped back excitedly. "Oh my God! You *are* going to meet them, aren't you? I was only joking this morning, but you're actually going to meet the Light Hunters."

Lux waved a dismissive hand.

"Because if you are, take me with you. I honestly can't stand another weekend sitting around while my sister tries to teach me algebra ..."

Lux looked past Maya. In the cabin, Ester was twisting in her seat, searching for him. Lux grimaced an apology.

"What?" asked Maya.

She turned and spotted Ester through the glass. She grinned and waved, pointing to Lux and making a can-you-believe-it face. Ester frowned.

"I do like Miss Hart," said Maya.

Before Lux could stop her, she'd yanked open the door to the main cabin. "Miss Hart," she called, "what a coincidence seeing you here."

Ester cast an anxious look around the cabin.

"I can't believe it. I just ran into Lux outside and . . ."

Ester leapt up and shoved Maya into the rear of the skybus, smiling reassuringly at her fellow travellers. Closing the door behind her, she guided Maya so she was against the window.

"You need to be quiet, now!" she growled.

Maya's smile melted from her face. She looked at Lux. "What's going on? Is everything okay?"

"Nothing's going on," said Ester quickly. "Nothing for you to worry about, anyway. All you have to do is go back into that cabin, sit in your seat and forget you've seen either of us."

Maya's cheeks had gone bright red. "I was only saying 'hi.' Tell her Lux . . ."

Lux didn't respond. He was staring at something outside the window – a fuzzy orange globe suspended in the black. At first, Lux thought it might be a hanging lamp on the outside of the skybus, but its hazy edge made him realise it must be further off. Was it a star? Or one of those lanterns people launched at birthday parties? He looked into the darkness. It was then Lux understood. The smudge wasn't a star or a lantern, or even a single light at all, but rather a string of five lights making up a half-moon. They grew by the second. Ester and Maya joined Lux and they all stared, mesmerised. The lights, Lux realised, belonged to another skyship.

The sky was such a large place, and skybuses so comparatively small, that in all his previous trips Lux had never encountered another ship outside of town. Ester opened the window wide and leaned out while Lux and Maya peered curiously over her shoulder. The lamps had grown so large now that the kids could make out the ship's hull. A dozen silhouetted figures lumbered upon the deck.

Suddenly, Ester froze, all the muscles in her forearms taut.

"What is it?" said Lux breathlessly.

"It's coming this way."

Lux laughed. Ester had to be kidding. But when she jabbed frantically at her Gauntlet, he examined the shape in the sky again. It took up almost the entire window now and was continuing to grow. Lux's mouth went instantly dry as he realised the ship wasn't *just* another skybus and Ester wasn't joking.

Heading directly for them was the largest skyship Lux had ever seen.

· CHAPTER 18 ·

Lux waited for the ship to adjust its trajectory. At first, it seemed to do just that, banking slowly left. But then his heart sank as it moved *closer* to them. The ship looked unreal, like it was part of a dream.

"That's him, isn't it?" he asked Ester worriedly.

"Who?" said Maya.

"I can't think of anyone else who'd fly so close to us," said Ester.

"How long do we have?" asked Lux.

"Who is it?" demanded Maya.

Ester studied the ship in the sky. "Twenty seconds."

Lux raced towards the main cabin, but Ester held him back. "What are you doing?" he shouted. "We have to tell them."

"There's no time."

"But . . ."

"We can't save them, Lux," said Ester firmly, "it's going to hit us." Ester waited for him to stop struggling and let go. Maya pulled him away as Ester inputted a series of quick commands into her Gauntlet. A small bubble of Light appeared, expanding until it engulfed all three of them.

"Was . . . was that a Gauntlet?" asked Maya incredulously.

Ester ignored her. "This should keep us safe. Both of you, get down."

With a final, frustrated look at the cabin, Lux did as he was told. Maya followed. Ester's Light cocoon had tinted everything around them blue, speckled with green blotches where the skybus lamps shone through. Lux looked at the main cabin. Why weren't people moving? Why weren't they doing something?

"We can't save them," Ester repeated.

"I'm scared," said Maya quietly.

Lux forced an encouraging smile and hung his head between his legs. The passage grew dark as the skyship closed in. Then it crashed, throwing Lux, Ester and Maya sideways into the Light barrier. The energy gave a little on contact, but not enough to protect them from the shock. Lux bumped his temple, sending a wave of dizziness through him. He fell to the ground, his ears ringing, as Maya and Ester did the same, their heads cracking on the wooden floor. Lux felt sick. His heart soared again when he saw Maya blink, even if Ester remained unconscious. Lux tried to crawl to her but was shunted aside as another crash rocked the ship. His hip hit the barrier and he cried out in pain.

Dragging himself up, Lux checked their status. The Light cocoon had held against the attack, but the skybus was catastrophically damaged. The windows were now a row of gaping holes. Glass littered the floor and the top of the Light barrier – one large, jagged piece balancing directly above Maya's head. Lux pushed her away from underneath it and crawled towards Ester.

"Lux, please tell me what's going on," cried Maya desperately.

"Not now!" snapped Lux.

Ester was still out cold. Lux shook her, but it was no good. He went to shake her again, but something stole his attention.

Through a gap in the frame he could see the attacking ship hovering menacingly in the sky. Lux could see a single porthole, and at the front a black figurehead – a rearing serpent with red eyes. A patch of smog by the porthole cleared and out of the dark swung four people, like little spiders on silky lines. They landed on the skybus. The sight of them almost made Lux choke. He shook Ester by the shoulders. Ahead, the four invaders braced themselves as the skybus shuddered.

A sudden realisation hit Lux. He and Maya would have to get out of Ester's Light bubble if they wanted to survive. Ignoring his pain, he sat up and beat the Light, encouraging Maya to do the same. But it was no good. The Light held. He reached for Ester's Gauntlet and frantically jabbed the buttons.

Nothing.

Lux was trembling now. He tried to wake Ester once more.

"Uh, Lux . . ." said Maya.

The woman at the front of the invaders – the one Lux had seen back in Daven by Deimos's cart – had lifted her lamp and was angling it towards him and Maya. They did their best to flatten themselves in the cramped space, but it was too late. The woman had seen them. She jerked a thumb in their direction and one by one the other invaders threaded their way towards them.

Lux got up and shook Ester with all the force he could muster. Why was she not waking? Ester murmured, breathing deeply, but still didn't come to. Deimos's people had reached the Light cocoon now. With no options, Lux shielded Maya at the back of the bubble.

The lady shone her lamp inside and peered through the smoky haze. She smirked menacingly. Pulling out a small, gun-shaped device, she aimed it at them, pressing the muzzle to the Light. Maya cringed. Lux watched as the lady raised three fingers on her free hand and snapped them slowly shut.

Three.

Two.

One.

Everything went black.

· CHAPTER 19 ·

Lux floated in and out of consciousness. One time, he opened his eyes to see the smirking lady in the overcoat and feel two heavy hands dragging him along. Another, he caught sight of the skybus, far away now, sputtering and flaming in the night sky. In another, he felt his shoes scrape across wooden decking as he squinted at a glowing, red Light engine.

Lux finally came to. He was immediately aware of a dull, humming sound. An engine? A biting wind cut through the noise, pinning his hair to his forehead. Instinctively, he tried to lift one of his hands to move it, but cold metal dug into his wrist.

Handcuffs.

Lux opened his eyes. He was on the deck of a large skyship. Maya was beside him, slumped on her feet, her hands behind her back. Ester was there too, studying the red haze emanating from the ship's engine as she struggled with her own cuffs. Noticing Lux was awake, she threw him a warning glance. A quick look told Lux what had spooked her – a small crowd of people in black overcoats. Deimos was at the front, opening and closing a dark metal lighter. He lit a cigar and gestured to one of his deputies. The girl brushed Lux's hair out of his eyes.

"It's a shame we've come to this," said Deimos as the girl retreated. He took a drag on his cigar and blew thick, grey smoke into the air. The smell reminded Lux of his grandpa. "A grave shame."

Ester spoke: "Don't tell him anything. Either of you."

"It seems your friend would rather we didn't chat," said Deimos, pacing the deck. "But I think there is no need for such unpleasantness." He reached behind Lux and Maya, unlocked their cuffs and resumed pacing. Lux flexed his wrists. "At least not between you and me.

"I'll be honest, I was hoping you'd join me of your own volition, Lux. Spirited though your . . . little acquaintance is," he looked admiringly at Maya, "it's you I'm after. However, if this is impossible, I will have to take you by force. You see, you really are too precious for me to leave behind."

"Why me?" asked Lux uncomprehendingly. "Why not Ester? Or anyone who can use Light?"

Deimos eyed Ester contemptuously. "Her? Oh no Lux, she's not like *us*." He waved a dismissive hand at her Gauntlet. "She might use her little *tricks* to do what we do, but she's not like *us*. People like you and I are rare."

Deimos took a final drag on his cigar and tossed it off the skyship. "But enough of this." He extended a muscular arm. A fan of red Light-daggers appeared at the end of his fingertips, shimmering and fizzing. "We could talk and talk, but it's action that turns the world. You are going to join me and you're going to do what you're told."

Deimos guided the knives so they were an inch from Ester's throat. Maya gasped. Ester clenched her jaw.

"Go on," she snarled, "see what happens."

Lux panicked. He tried to think of something to deflect Deimos. "I-I-I don't want to go with you!" he blurted, pulling back on Deimos's forearm. Deimos held firm. "My grandpa said you were dangerous."

Deimos dismissed his daggers. "Your grandpa? It was *because* of your grandpa that this world is as it is. Your grandpa is a fool."

Lux bunched his fists and fought an urge to lash out. He opened his mouth to argue but something Deimos had said stopped him. Grandpa. His grandpa had made the world what it is.

"What do you mean, my grandpa?"

"Ignore him," said Ester.

Deimos studied Lux wearily. "Your grandpa is not the man you think he is, Lux."

Lux's legs buckled beneath him. What was he talking about? What did he mean? Over his shoulder, Lux heard Ester's voice.

"Lux, Maya, when I say jump, jump!"

A small Light orb appeared at Ester's feet. She kicked it across to Deimos's people. Deimos saw the Light and fixed Ester with an admiring expression. Waving a hand, he enclosed himself in an sphere of red energy. Ester dropped her cuffs, gathered Lux and Maya in a bearhug and leapt towards the gunwale. Lux caught sight of Ester's orb, which had landed by the smirking woman from the skybus. It seemed to implode slightly and then exploded in a violent outpouring of Light. The blast blew a hole in the deck, scattering Deimos's agents. It hit Lux, Ester and Maya a moment later, hurling them through the side of the skyship.

The last thing Lux saw, as they tumbled to the ground thousands of metres below, was Deimos hovering safely in his ball of Light.

· CHAPTER 20 ·

The world spun around Lux, rushing by in a blur of greys and blacks and blues. He could hear the wind howling violently and see juddering orange hairlines as Deimos's burning skyship turned lazily into view. Below, Ester and Maya were revolving end on end, so that Lux saw first their heads, then their boots, then their heads again. Ester jerked her arms, desperately trying to stop her spinning.

Beneath Lux was a chasm of darkness. It prompted a strange feeling in him, like he was falling in a dream. Tucking his elbows to his hips, he manoeuvred so he was falling face-first and immediately gained speed, cutting through the air like an arrow. Ester had shifted now so she was no longer spinning, and she'd managed to grab Maya, so they were falling together.

Ester inched Maya out of the way and spread her arms, giving Lux as large a space as possible to aim for. They came together with a thump. Ester gripped his jacket to stop him bouncing away, but the jolt had forced one of Maya's arms out and restarted their tumbling. Lux tried to stop this even as he fought to keep hold of Ester's waist.

His head was just below Ester's chin now, so he had to be careful to avoid butting her. She jabbed at her Gauntlet. The machine expelled wisps of Light that dissipated agonisingly into the black.

"How long do we have?" said Lux.

"Not long enough!" shouted Ester.

Lux saw the faint orange blur of a town or village beneath them. It was hard to tell how close they were to the ground, but he figured they couldn't have much further to go. He looked again at Ester's Gauntlet, which hissed and spluttered. He prayed for it to work. As if in answer, a ribbon of blue-white Light appeared from the end, expanding in the dark. It mushroomed into a parachute and Lux felt a sudden tug as the Light-mesh caught the air.

But rather than joy he saw fear on Ester's face.

Immediately Lux's mind leapt to Deimos. Was he back on their trail? But it wasn't Deimos. Lux looked up and saw a narrow slash in the Light-parachute's canopy, peeling rapidly apart. The last wisps of Light at the chute's edges faded, throwing them into darkness. All the hairs on Lux's neck stood up. Ester jabbed desperately at her Gauntlet, before giving up and growling in defeat.

"Can't someone *do* something?" shouted Maya. She flapped her hands, trying to slow them down. She reached for Lux to do the same.

But he ignored her.

In his mind, he was back in Daven, hearing his grandpa calling him clumsy for dropping yet another expensive watch to the workshop floor. Lux's grandpa had taught him a cast to remedy this: *Catch*. It involved creating a Light cushion under a falling object. Lux had been slow to grasp it, but in time he'd become so quick at performing the cast that he was able to drop an antique watch and have a *Catch* waiting before it hit the floor. It wasn't healing, really – just a little Light-trick – but it had proven useful. He thought of it now as they fell. Would it work? Would he be able to cast it while falling? He'd never tried to catch anything bigger than a teacup ...

Lux pushed Ester and Maya away. He concentrated on breathing slowly, trying to control his racing heart. Tension built in his arms and threads of blue Light issued from his fingers. Was he getting it right? Normally, Lux could have thrown the cast in his sleep, but now ... As the ground rushed towards them, he poured all his remaining energy into the Light, and soon it coalesced into a large sphere. He guided it so it was beneath them. By this point Ester had worked out his plan and she urged him on.

"Yes! Yes! Go on!"

Lux took a last, hopeful breath and let go. They hit the ground a moment later, slamming into the *Catch* so that Lux, Ester and Maya were completely submerged in blue Light. Then they were out, trampolining into the sky. When they dropped again, Lux thudded into the hard, dusty ground. The impact knocked the wind out of him as Maya and Ester landed a few paces off. They each rolled in the gravel, gasping for breath. Lux's *Catch* imploded and it was dark again.

"Remind me," said Maya groggily, "next time I visit my sister . . . to bring a parachute."

· CHAPTER 21 ·

Lux lay on the ground, his body cradled by a leafy bush. Deimos's skyship floated steadily across the sky, fires spreading as it shrank in the distance. The ship dwindled until it was no bigger than a star, then disappeared behind a mountain.

There was no sign of the Lindhelm skybus.

Lux sat up. They'd landed in the middle of a valley near the village. A cracked, dusty road connected the village to the mountains. Next to Maya was a squat, bare tree. An old, wooden cart lay abandoned beside it, one wheel smashed and the other poking out of the dirt. A light breeze whistled softly by.

Ester rose wearily, moaning as she shifted her weight. She looked from the village to the mountains. Satisfied they were alone, she hobbled to the cart, planting her right foot carefully.

"I think we've lost them," she announced, "but we shouldn't dawdle. Come on. Get up."

Get up? Lux didn't feel like going anywhere. All those people on the skybus ... Why would anyone do such a thing?

Neither Lux nor Maya moved. Ester yanked a loose wooden panel off the cart and snapped it in half with her good foot, creating two strips as wide as her leg. She positioned one under her armpit and tested her weight. The crutch held.

"Come on," she called out impatiently.

Lux swung his head slowly around, his eyes red and puffy. "What did he mean about my grandpa, Ester? He said grandpa was to blame. To blame for what?"

Ester studied the road to the mountains. She didn't answer.

"Did he do something wrong?" Lux's voice grew louder.

Ester limped to Lux, sank onto an upturned rock and balanced her crutch against her knee. "Listen, I don't know what Deimos meant, but I do know one lesson life has taught me: you've got to make your own decisions. Do you think your grandpa's a bad man?"

"No."

"Then he's not. But what *is* bad is our position out here on this road. We might have lost Deimos, but he knows where we came down. It won't be long until he sends someone. We have to move. Speaking of quick moves," added Ester, "impressive *Catch* back there. Without you, we'd have been pancakes."

Lux shrugged.

"Perhaps our Luminary was right about you after all." Ester

struggled to her feet. "But we'll find that out in time. For now, we should get going."

"What about me?" said Maya. "What am I supposed to do? I ... I don't even know what's happening. First, I was on the skybus ... then those ... those people came ..." Her eyes welled. "You need to tell me what's happening. Who *were* they? Why have you got that thing on your arm?"

"I'm sorry, Maya," Ester replied, crossing the road. "You were never supposed to be involved in any of this. Best thing you can do is go home." She pointed to the village. "Go to those houses. Tell them who you are."

Lux shifted on his feet. "Ester ..."

"Lux, we can't take her with us. We're going to be slow enough as it is." She rubbed her injured ankle. "It's best for everyone, especially Maya, if she goes to the village."

"What if Deimos comes for her?"

Maya looked up quickly. "Is that the man on the ship?" She grabbed Ester's arm. "Please don't leave me if he's coming. Please take me with you."

"Do you even know where we're going? You wouldn't be so keen if you did."

"I don't care," cried Maya desperately. "Just don't leave me for ... *him*."

Ester sighed.

"I don't think we should leave her," said Lux. "If Deimos finds her, she'll be able to tell him exactly where we're going."

"She won't," said Ester. "She doesn't know."

Lux frowned. "I can't leave her, Ester. She's my best friend."

Ester thought. "Lux, it's up to you. My job is to get you to Dawnstar. If that means bringing Maya . . ." She shrugged. "But don't blame me if it goes wrong. I was only meant to rescue you."

Lux took Maya's arm and guided her across the road. "Maya," he whispered, "something bad happened today. We had to leave Daven. It wasn't a choice. You can come with us, but that man back there is dangerous. Maybe you *would* be safer going back to Daven. But you've got to decide now. We can't wait."

"I want to come."

"You're sure?"

Maya shrugged. "If I'm in danger either way, I'd rather be with my best friend." Her eyes twinkled.

Lux hugged her. Ester looked up from her Gauntlet. "So?"

"She's going to come."

· CHAPTER 22 ·

"What about your leg?" Lux nodded at Ester's injured ankle. "Do you want me to throw a *Heal*?"

"You think a bump like that would stop a Light Hunter?"

Maya jerked at the mention of the Hunters. She looked quickly at Lux, but he put up a hand to say 'not now.' In truth, Ester's reference to the Hunters made Lux feel better too. If Ester really was a Light Hunter, then he and Maya were in good hands.

"So, where are we going?" he asked, combing twigs out of his hair.

Ester climbed a rock near the upended cart. "If there's one thing you'll learn about the Light Hunters, it's that we never do anything without a plan. If Deimos hadn't rammed us when he did, we'd have been jumping from the skybus anyway."

Lux recoiled. "Jumping?"

Ester waited for him to figure it out. When he didn't, she rolled her eyes.

"Your grandpa had it dead-on when he called you a dipstick." She hobbled to Lux, wrapped an arm around him and pointed at the mountains. "We were heading for the Light Hunter HQ, yes?"

"Excuse me?" said Maya. Her eyebrows shot up.

Lux nodded.

"And we were going to jump from the skybus?" said Ester.

"Did you just say Light Hunters HQ?" asked Maya incredulously.

"Yes!" said Ester.

At once, Maya started to hyperventilate, pacing across the road. "She can't have said what I think she said."

Lux was doing his best not to look too excited, but the idea that Dawnstar might be this close to his hometown made him feel giddy too. If Ester had said a local branch of the Light Hunters, Lux might have understood. Aside from Daven and Kofi, most towns still had an outpost or two tucked away somewhere. But Dawnstar's location was one of the world's great mysteries. Ordinarily, with such secrets, *somebody* found out. How could they not? People always let secrets slip. But Lux had never heard so much as a rumour that Dawnstar was nearby. Could it really be true?

"Oh my word," said Maya, still reeling. "You're not having us on, are you?"

"I wouldn't be too excited," said Ester, grinning. "We keep Dawnstar's location such a secret that even us Light Hunters don't know *exactly* where it is. We usually use our Gauntlets to get us there, but . . ." She presented the device's charred remains.

"You must have some idea," said Lux hopefully.

"Oh, I know it's in the Tartas mountains, but where . . ." Ester trailed off, peering up at the soaring peaks.

Maya looked inquisitively at the Gauntlet. "How does this help then?"

"We'll just have to hike into the mountains," said Ester, "and hope I recognise something."

Maya frowned, a little hurt that Ester had ignored her. "Seriously, how does it work?"

"This is a highly sensitive piece of equipment," said Ester sharply, losing her patience. "It can manipulate Light. It's not something you can just explain to a twelve-year-old . . ."

Maya, who'd been circling Ester and examining the gadget, turned to Lux. "There's a capacitor there that links to some kind of engine inside." She bit her lip, thinking. "If its connecting field has enough charge . . ." She tried to touch the Gauntlet, but Ester snatched it away.

"Maya, if you're going to come along, I need you to be quiet."

"You should listen to her," Lux told Ester. "She knows what she's talking about."

"She knows Light Hunter tech?"

"She knows about every other piece of tech ever invented."

Ester looked long and hard at Maya. "If I let you touch this, you have to be exceptionally careful. One wrong move could set off a Light-explosion that'll kill everyone in this valley."

"Trust her," urged Lux.

Ester unstrapped the Gauntlet and handed it over. Maya slumped onto a nearby rock and prodded and pulled at the dark-chrome gadget, muttering, "Ah, I see," and "Oh, that's so weird."

"Careful," warned Ester as Maya tugged a wire free from the machine's casing.

"Do you locate Dawnstar with a kind of proximity location system?" Maya asked.

"Yes." Ester cocked her head, surprised.

"Thought so." Maya hunched over the gadget again. "I think its central engine's gone, which is why that parachute thing vanished when we fell."

"It's dead then?" said Lux. He didn't like the sound of that.

"I didn't say that."

Maya adjusted the machine – at one point pulling a thin screwdriver out of her back pocket and carefully scraping away some ash and soot. When she was done, she handed the device back to Ester.

"No good?"

"Not as whatever you normally use it for," said Maya. "But I fixed the HQ-locator thing."

Ester cast a wary look at Lux.

"Try it," he said.

Ester strapped the battered Gauntlet to her wrist and fiddled with a couple of dials. A beep sounded.

"Is that it?" Lux was aware of Maya grinning beside him. "Is that the locator?"

"It is, isn't it?" blurted Maya excitedly. "I reckon they didn't want to put a map on the device in case you lose it and anyone finds it."

Ester listened to the chirp. She smiled.

"I knew it!" said Maya.

Lux pumped his fist. "So, we can get to Dawnstar?"

"We can," said Ester. "And we'd better go." She eyed Maya with a newfound look of admiration, then hopped off the rock and paced away.

Lux and Maya watched her – one moment studying the starry night sky, the next listening to her Gauntlet. Maya sighed. "Skyship crashes, falling from the sky, Light Hunters, a Gauntlet . . ." Her eyes lit up, ". . . that *I* fixed." She raised her eyebrows. "I must be dreaming."

Lux laughed. "You're not, but you could probably do with a bit of an explanation. Come on. I'll tell you on the way."

· CHAPTER 23 ·

A shallow river zig-zagged across the valley tracing the same path Deimos's craft had taken through the sky. Ester hurried towards it, stopping every few paces to listen to the beep at her wrist. Eventually, they left the road. As they walked, Lux told Maya everything – how his grandpa had taught him to throw Light, that Ester was a Light Hunter, how Lux had run into Deimos on the beach and how Deimos had tried to kidnap him.

"And all the other kids at the orphanage thought you were boring!" Maya exclaimed with a mocking twinkle in her eye.

The river flowed swiftly downstream, accompanied by awkward crags and rocks. Lux and Maya helped Ester over the worst of them, hauling her up particularly steep ledges or holding her crutch as she shuffled down.

"Is it taking us the right way?" Lux indicated the Gauntlet.

"I think so," said Ester. "I'm starting to recognise some of the land. I should find it if I keep my eyes peeled."

Soon, the river dipped around an overhanging rocky ledge and twisted out of sight. As they tracked the beeping signal, Lux noticed a handful of odd-looking trees, their willowy silhouettes swaying creepily in the dull light.

"We're here," said Ester. She hobbled to a tree that stood apart from the rest, its drooping branches creating a wide curtain. "What I'm about to show you is something nobody outside of the Light Hunters has ever seen. You can't tell anybody."

Ester's steady gaze communicated her seriousness. Lux and Maya nodded.

Ester leaned her crutch against a tree and groaned as she sank into a squat, feeling all around the tree's roots. Lux heard a click and to his surprise a perfect square of yellow light appeared in the ground, revealing a descending, lantern-lit staircase. Lux and Maya gazed down in wonder, pinching their noses against an unpleasant musty smell. Ester retrieved her crutch and made her way down.

"Well," she said daringly, "are you coming?"

The passage was marginally taller than Ester, so that Lux and Maya could walk comfortably but Ester had to stoop to avoid banging her head. Their footsteps echoed off the stone. Lux touched one of the walls, coating his fingertips in feathery dust. He slowed so he was walking alongside Maya. She looked like she hadn't slept for a week.

"Are you all right?"

Maya thought. "Yes. No. Yes. I think." She laughed feebly. "This isn't quite how I expected this weekend to go. I reckon my sister's probably having a heart attack wondering where I am. But yes, I think I'm all right. You?"

Lux opened his mouth to say yes, then realised he wasn't sure. He'd barely thought about his own safety at all since leaving Daven. Even now, his mind tumbled with thoughts of his grandpa. Deimos had been heading to the old man's workshop. Surely, he'd have found him. His grandpa was too ill to defend himself. And Deimos's words back on the skyship haunted Lux. His grandpa was to blame. For what? What could he possibly have done?

"I think I'm okay," he said. "I'm just worried about grandpa. What if they found him back in Daven?"

"Your grandpa survived the Cerberus attack," said Maya flatly. "I'm sure he can handle old ashy-hair Deimos."

Lux chuckled. He was happy Maya had some of her pep back.

Just then, an ice-cold draught whipped down the tunnel. Quite unexpectedly, Lux heard rustling leaves. A staircase appeared, leading to the surface. Ester climbed up, placing weight gingerly on her right foot and gripping the wall to steady herself. A hatch at the top was already half-open. Poking her head outside, Ester viewed the surrounding land and then clumped back down. Wedging her crutch under her armpit, she motioned for Lux and Maya to follow.

· CHAPTER 24 ·

They emerged onto a wide, grey plateau ringed by a steep wall as high as Daven's Monster watchtowers. The wall framed a circle of black sky. Boulders dotted the plain – some as small as Lux, others bigger than his grandpa's workshop. The tallest was at the plateau's centre. Lux spun, taking in his surroundings. It was like being in a volcano.

"No," said Ester flatly.

"No what?"

"It's not a volcano."

Lux stared at her, amazed. Could Light Hunters read minds?

"It's what I thought when I first saw it," Ester explained.

"What is it then?" asked Maya. "It's not normal."

"It's a meteor crater."

"Really?"

"So Tesla thinks."

"Tesla?" Maya stopped walking. "*The* Tesla?"

"Who's Tesla?" asked Lux, puzzled.

Maya flicked him hard on the forehead. "Tesla's only the greatest Inventor in history."

Lux felt silly. He thought he knew all there was to know about Light Hunters, but clearly he didn't know as much as Maya.

"Don't worry," said Ester encouragingly, seeing Lux's face, "you'll meet him."

"When did it hit?" asked Maya.

"A few thousand years ago. A meteor called Korat. Smashed into the mountains and carved out this bowl. Dawnstar's on the other side."

Ester pointed to a distant wall that was almost entirely black, apart from an inverted, blue glowing triangle halfway along. *Must be some kind of Light shield,* thought Lux. As he stared, a far-off rumble sounded, making Maya jump.

Thunder.

Lux held out a hand. No rain yet but he wanted to get to Dawnstar before the storm rolled in. He shouldered his backpack and walked. "Come on."

Ester smirked and followed. They picked their way through dozens of boulders, the crater floor undulating beneath them so that one minute they were trudging up a steady slope, breathing heavily, and the next ambling downhill, as if they were strolling on a sunny day.

Presently, they reached the crater's central peak, where Lux helped Ester over a nasty set of rocks. They rested on a small boulder as they waited for Maya to catch up.

"Hooo! I'm not as fit as I thought," Maya huffed, when she finally arrived.

Lux had a good view of the Light Hunters HQ now, which had grown considerably since he'd first seen it – the blue light sharper, clearer. Too small to be the entirety of Dawnstar, it had to be some kind of entrance.

The journey down the central peak was easier on Ester's ankle, and she hummed absently as they walked. Cutting into this every now and then was the rumble Lux had heard earlier, a deep, earthy growl that made him flinch. He'd hated storms since his grandpa had taken him on a hiking trip into the Daven countryside for his sixth birthday and they'd got caught in a cataclysmic thunderstorm. So terrifying were the slamming bolts, and so wild were the winds that whipped the trees, that the incident had left Lux scarred. Back in the crater, he hurried forwards.

"Can we go faster please?" he called to Ester and Maya.

In time, a wide crack in the ground forced them to veer around a large boulder. A second rock, resting at a forty-five-degree angle, formed a natural barrier. Lux looked to see if they could get around it, but it was no good. They'd have to crawl through a narrow gap at the bottom.

"I'll go first," said Ester.

She sank to her knees and tossed her crutch through. Lux gestured for Maya to go next, and then followed. When they re-emerged, he froze.

Another rumble.

Only now it was clear the sound was not a thunderstorm, but rather that it was coming from *inside* the crater. Lux tried to locate its source. Could it have been a falling boulder? Or maybe a tree? The sound came again and this time he had it.

He gasped.

The blue smudge of Light.

What before Lux had taken to be an unbroken mass, he now saw was made up of five distinct sections – two thin wedges below, a thick central trunk and two long wedges either side. To his amazement, the whole lot seemed to be rocking left and right. Buried in the middle were two massive, milky white orbs, each containing a red oval and black dot. Lux stared, trying to work out what they were.

And then it hit him.

The rumbling and the lumbering . . . He wasn't staring at a shield. Or a building. It was a building-sized creature. And the enormous white orbs, though it made Lux dizzy to think it, were its eyes.

· CHAPTER 25 ·

"That's a . . . Monster."

Maya looked. "*What..?*"

Lux searched for Ester, his heart pounding. What was she playing at, leading them to a Monster?

The creature's mouth yawned and belched a glowing orange orb into the air. At first, the shape was too far away for Lux to see what it was. But as it travelled inwards from the crater's edge, he realised, with a start, it was a fireball.

Lux's head spun. He scanned his surroundings frantically for somewhere to hide and spied a large, potato-shaped boulder to his right.

"Over there!" he yelled to Maya.

He searched for Ester and found her leaning calmly on her

crutch, gazing at the Monster. Racing over, he tugged her towards Maya, but Ester shrugged him off.

"Come on!" he shouted.

Ester smiled serenely. Something about her lack of panic made Lux pause. He looked again at the beast, which was stamping its feet angrily, steam pouring out of its nostrils. And yet, now Lux looked more closely, he could see the steam had a strange bluish tint to it. Just like Light.

It hit him.

Why Ester didn't seem bothered by the creature. Why she was happy to stand in front of it as if she was doing nothing more dangerous than queuing for a newspaper. She had no need to be afraid.

"That's not real, is it?" Lux shouted.

"Would I be standing here if it was?"

Lux fetched Maya. He realised, without Ester telling him, that the Monster was some kind of projection – a Light hologram. Lux felt no embarrassment; he'd never seen Light used in this way before. It seemed so *real*. Even now he knew it was fake, it was still hard to believe. He could *see* steam venting from the Monster's nostrils, could feel the ground shudder as it rocked on its feet.

"Are you telling me that's not a Monster?" said Maya disbelievingly.

"It's a Guardian," explained Ester. "A Light projection from inside Dawnstar. Keeps people away."

"Why didn't you tell us?" demanded Lux.

"Lux," said Ester, regarding him, "you might be pretty good at throwing Light. Heck, people smarter than me are risking a lot to secure your abilities. But if you want to fit in here, you're going to have to get used to this kind of thing."

Ester held Lux's gaze until he looked away, then headed towards the projection. Excited though he was to see Dawnstar, a part of Lux wanted to shout that he *didn't* want to get used to this stuff. That really he wanted to go back to Daven, to his grandpa. But he knew Ester was right. For now, his destination was Dawnstar.

Taking a deep breath, he jogged after her. "Come on," he said brightly, "I thought we were in a hurry."

Up close, the Light Guardian was even more convincing than it had been from afar. Lux felt like he could *smell* the beast – grease and rotting meat. It stood on two powerful legs that ended in razor-sharp claws, and its torso was as big as a skybus. Its snouted, fanged head dripped gobs of simulated saliva. Lux flinched as the Guardian's eyes turned on him. It reared, ready to attack. Only by looking at Ester, who was standing casually by the Guardian's other claw, was Lux able to calm down.

Ester hobbled towards the creature's leg, planting her crutch wearily. The Guardian noticed her just as she was about pass through. A thunderous roar exploded from its throat and it slammed a paw into Ester, turning her skin a translucent grey. Ester continued as if nothing had happened, limping out the other side. Lux squeezed his eyes shut and slipped through while the Guardian's focus was still on Ester. His skin prickled. *Was there really no easier way into Dawnstar?*

When Lux opened his eyes again, he nearly jumped. Instead

of the wall he'd seen before, the crater floor now rose up, giving way to a wide, stone staircase, flanked by polished towers. Square, boxy buildings stood either side, their windows glinting in the moonlight. Dotted amongst them were craggy overhangs, ribboned with balconies.

"Whoa!" said Maya.

"Is this..?" started Lux.

"Yes," said Ester grandly, "welcome to Dawnstar."

"So, the crater wall . . .?"

"Another projection," confirmed Ester. "It'd be no good frightening people off if they could see the HQ right behind it."

Maya's eyes devoured the sight. "It's . . . amazing."

"We can't take all the credit," said Ester. "Dawnstar's built around a collection of ruins that have been here a very long time."

"Ruins?" Lux peeled his eyes from the HQ.

"We've found some fascinating Light tech in the depths." Ester lifted her burnt Gauntlet. "That's where this thing comes from. You'll have to ask Tesla if you want to know more."

Lux chuckled, amazed. For years, he and Maya had played Light Hunters on their school playground, hiding from dinner ladies to avoid being told off. Now they were *at* Dawnstar. Was he dreaming? Maya looked like she was about to burst with excitement. Lux sprinted to the staircase and planted a boot on the stone, checking it was real and not another illusion. He jumped to the next step. *This is it,* he thought, *this is really Dawnstar.* His insides were tingling. He'd never seen anything like it. Ester struggled to catch up.

"You've not been out of town before, have you?" she said to Lux.

"I've been to Kofi," he said, "and a few places on school trips. But apart from that . . ." He gazed at the stony, glittering scene, shaking his head in amazement. "Dawnstar . . ."

"Yes," said Ester, seeing her home fresh for the first time in years. "Come on," she jabbed her crutch playfully into his side, "it's time we went home."

· CHAPTER 26 ·

Lux counted a hundred-and-fifty steps to where the staircase finally met the crater wall – long, wearying strides that burned his thighs. From the floor, the steps had seemed to disappear where they met the rock, but now Lux saw that they continued *into* the crater wall. He and Maya skipped on as the rock closed around them, swallowing them up, until they found themselves climbing in near darkness. Maya darted ahead. A moment later, Lux heard her excited voice echoing off the stone.

"Lux, come here. You've got to see this!"

Ignoring his aching calves, Lux bolted up and reached a large, stone platform. Ester caught up with them a minute later, breathing heavily. She handed her crutch to Maya and stepped forward.

At the far end of the platform was a wall, decorated with an archway. In the centre Lux could see a star-shaped recess. Ester lifted her hand and pressed on one of her rings. A Light-image of a star appeared above it. She slotted it into the recess – the Light scraping noisily on the stone. Lux heard a low, rumbling hum as the wall disappeared, replaced by a bright, cyan-blue window of Light.

"Welcome," said Ester, stepping sideways through the opening, "to Dawnstar."

Lux and Maya slid through after her and promptly froze. They'd arrived at a vast, brightly-lit atrium. Dozens of people hurried past – some carrying clipboards, some cleaning buckets and mops, others piles of uniforms, and yet more carrying unfamiliar contraptions and tools. Rows of rooms climbed to the ceiling, filled with yet more people. Two Light-powered elevators motored up and down at the atrium's corners. Another enormous Light Guardian occupied the space between, this one motionless. Hundreds of sketched images plastered the walls – Dawnstar, famous Light Hunters, Monsters.

Lux wondered whether there was a Cerberus and stepped towards them. As he did, a movement at his feet caught his eye. The floor was *reacting* to his steps. Wispy tendrils of blue Light curled around his toes where they touched the ground. Lux gazed fascinatedly at the ripples, narrowly avoiding a woman carrying a conjured pair of Light-scissors. She shot him a warning glance.

"There'll be time for that later," said Ester, nodding at the pictures. "First we have to report in."

Report in? Lux thought. *To who?* He allowed Ester to lead him away.

A passing boy in a mauve uniform saluted Ester smartly. Ester stopped him, unstrapped her charred Gauntlet and handed it over. "Take that to Tesla," she said, flexing her forearm, "tell him Ester says sorry. Again."

The boy grimaced.

They cut through the crowds towards the Guardian, Maya pointing out anything interesting she saw as they went. Ester made a beeline for one of the Light elevators. Lux noticed he and Maya were dressed differently to everyone else there, who wore the fitted mauve uniform or battle-gear like Ester's. People were staring and Lux did his best to appear friendly, grinning bashfully at his tatty trousers and faded t-shirt. At the elevator, an attendant saluted and lifted the metal rail. Ester thanked her and led Lux and Maya inside. A couple tried to join them, but Ester shook her head and they slunk away.

Ester punched a button and the elevator rose. Lux stared into the atrium, trying to count the number of floors. Was it five? Or six? Maybe seven? He decided there were too many and gave up.

"Who is it we're going to see?" he asked curiously.

"The man who's going to protect you from Deimos," said Ester simply.

Lux was about to ask her for more, but the Light elevator slowed to a stop and a second attendant poked her face inside. She smiled warmly and retracted the rail. Lux thanked her before hurrying after Ester.

For the next few minutes, she guided Lux and Maya through Dawnstar. First came the Light-lit corridors, each with its own coloured variation of Light-lamps to help the Hunters navigate their labyrinth home. The corridors were covered with yet more sketches – Hunters and Monsters, as well as Light-casts. They passed classrooms, in which uniformed youngsters practised Light casts, overseen by older Hunters. They passed workshops that reminded Lux of his grandpa's, where overall-wearing mechanics hunched over wooden benches, using Light-tools to repair odd contraptions. They skirted cavernous, echoing skyship hangars and poked their heads into Dawnstar's kitchens, dorms, libraries and bathrooms.

"Can you pinch me?" Lux asked Maya excitedly.

"Only if you pinch *me*."

Finally, they reached a courtyard where a skylight framed a view of the stars. Lux, Ester and Maya crossed it in silence. At the end, a porch stood nestled beneath a handsome building decorated with hanging flowers. Lux was just about to ask Ester where they were when she spoke.

"The man you're about to meet is the most important person in this place," she said seriously. "Only speak if he asks you a question. Especially you, Maya. Remember, you're not even supposed to be here."

Lux and Maya nodded.

Ester neatened her clothes and opened the door.

"Hi Dad," she called, her voice light in a way it hadn't been since she and Lux had left his grandpa's workshop, "I'm home."

· CHAPTER 27 ·

Lux blinked. Had he heard that right? Had she really said "dad?" Or were his ears playing tricks on him? Dad. He looked at Maya and whispered the word.

They'd entered a lavishly-decorated room unlike the others at Dawnstar. Gone were the Guardians and Light-floors, replaced by mahogany furniture and oak floorboards. Tall bookcases, filled with faded, dusty hardbacks, overlooked a weapon rack showcasing an assortment of swords. The room smelled old and antique, like the museum Lux's grandpa took him to back in Daven. A second red door at the rear – wedged open by a bronze Monster statue – let in explosive flashes of Light. Outside, a balcony overlooked another courtyard. There, his shadow growing and shrinking when the Light flared, was Artello Nova.

The years had done little to change Nova, who was still the same barrel-chested man Lux had seen in his sister's Light Hunter books. His hair was full, and tied in a neat, braided pony-tail. His forehead was creased, accompanied now by thin lines at the lips. He was clean-shaven and wore the same heavy gear that lay somewhere between everyday clothes and armour. Over this, he wore a pale-blue robe, his left arm resting in it like a sling – an injury long rumoured to have been sustained during a Monster battle gone wrong.

A sense of relief swept through Nova when he heard Ester's voice. He leaned over the balcony. "That'll be all for today. We'll continue training tomorrow. Dismissed."

Lux heard footsteps pound the courtyard. Nova shut the door behind him and rushed forward, gathering up Ester in a hug. "Good to see you, my girl," he said happily. "It has been too long."

"Too long," Ester agreed.

Nova saw Lux and Maya, still standing in the doorway. "I presume this young man is Lux Dowd?"

"We've come from Daven tonight," said Ester.

"And who is the girl?" said Nova, shifting his piercing gaze to Maya.

Ester sighed. "It's a long story."

"My name's Maya."

Nova regarded Maya, then his daughter. "You said you came from Daven tonight?" He rubbed his chin in thought. "Deimos?"

Ester collapsed onto one of the sofas and undid her combat belt. "Yes. He's been hanging around town the last few days. He moved tonight. We barely got away."

Nova studied Lux closely, so that he felt a little hot and anxious. He couldn't tell whether Nova was happy or angry. Lux flinched as the old man crossed the room. He stopped in front of Lux and extended a hand. Lux hesitated.

"I am Artello Nova," he said, taking Lux's hand, "the Luminary here. Ester is my daughter. I am sorry we had to bring you in as we did. We did not expect Deimos to move so soon." Nova shook Maya's hand.

"I am certain you have lots of questions. And I will answer them. But you two look like you need a sit down." Nova showed Lux and Maya to a sofa and gestured for Ester to walk with him to the other side of the room. There, they held a hushed conference.

"Please tell me that's not the real Artello Nova," whispered Maya.

Lux nudged her away. He was trying to focus on Ester and Nova.

"Honestly," said Maya, almost dizzy with excitement, "I think getting on that skybus was the best thing I ever did."

When Nova and Ester returned, Ester snapped a finger for Maya to follow. "Come on, we're leaving."

"I can't. I have to keep an eye on Lux."

"Maya . . ."

She tried to argue but Lux stopped her. "It's all right. I'll be fine. I'll see you in a bit."

Reluctantly, Maya trudged after Ester.

Alone with Lux now, Nova fetched a heaping plate of sandwiches from his desk, took a cheese one and offered the rest to Lux. "You do not have to ask," he said. "This is your home now."

The thought hit Lux like a tsunami. All the excitement and fear of the chase – the skyships, crashes, secret tunnels and Guardians – all of it had kept him going. But now that they'd reached Dawnstar, it all became too much. Nova was right. For now, this *was* Lux's home. Tears began to stream down his cheeks, puffing up his eyes. Nova fetched a wooden chair from his desk and sat in front of Lux. He allowed him to cry, sipping slowly from a glass of water.

Finally, Lux sat back on the sofa, his face red.

Nova smiled warmly. "We all need a good cry every now and then. But after a while the time for crying passes and the time for action comes."

"Action?" Lux frowned, trying to make sense of what he was hearing. What did Nova mean? "I don't even understand why I'm here. I don't know what's happening. One second everything's fine, then my housekeeper's a Light Hunter. And a man called Deimos is after me!"

Nova nodded. "I suppose I do owe you an explanation." He took the plate of sandwiches and held it out once more. Lux picked a ham one.

"How are you with heights?" asked Nova casually.

Lux looked puzzled.

"Never mind," said Nova, waving away his own question. "We need to go up anyway." He tilted his head to look at the ceiling. "Take us up."

At once, all the lamps in Nova's room dimmed and a low hum rumbled under Lux's feet. It grew in intensity, until it became a loud, mechanical hiss. A circular section of the floor detached from the rest and rose up as the ceiling peeled away. Through the gap, a glass dome presented a view of the night sky. The mechanism clicked loudly and stopped. They'd arrived in some kind of observatory. Lux got up and ran his hand along the glass, staring at the stars.

"This is . . ."

"I know," said Nova, anticipating Lux's response. "But we are not here to stargaze." He motioned for Lux to sit back on the sofa. "Settle in, young man. This is likely to be quite a tale."

· CHAPTER 28 ·

"Tell me what you know of the Monster attack that killed your family."

Lux's breath caught in his throat. He didn't like talking about that night. "Why are you asking?"

"It is important, Lux. Tell me."

Lux looked down. "I know what everyone knows. It was a Cerberus. It attacked Daven ten years ago, killed hundreds and destroyed the town. It got away." A hazy image of Lux's family appeared in his mind. "I lost my parents and my sister."

"What of the Light Hunters?"

"I know people blame them for what happened. But I don't believe it. Neither does my grandpa." Lux shrugged defiantly. "I don't care if it's banned or not, I don't think throwing Light's bad."

"I see." Nova took a small device from a slot in the dome and pressed a button. A curved image appeared on the glass. As the black and white shapes crystallised, Lux recognised it as a picture of Daven. Except unlike any image he'd ever seen, this one was moving.

"How?"

"It is a Light-projector," said Nova. "It shows things from the past."

Things from the past? How could anything show things from the past? "That's . . . amazing."

"We had two warnings of Monster attacks that night," said Nova, ignoring Lux's excitement. "One in Ringtown, and one in Daven. Back then, we had Light Hunters posted in every town, ready to get a message to us whenever a Monster attacked; the size of it, how many there were, all we needed to know. But something went wrong that night. Messages got mixed up. Our Luminary at the time sent most of his Hunters to Ringtown, thinking their attack the more severe, and only a single squad to Daven."

Lux peered at the image, which seemed to be from the viewpoint of the lighthouse. At the bottom he could see the harbour, and beyond that the Monster statues on the promenade. *No Cerberus*, he noted. Something else caught his attention in the bottom-right corner of the image – a dark shadow, skulking through shallow water.

"By the time we got there, the Cerberus had destroyed most of the southern part of town."

The dark shape emerged, its matted fur glistening in the moonlight. The Cerberus had three large heads, each as big as a skybus and armed with oily tongues and razor-sharp teeth.

Lux watched it mount the promenade, snapping at anyone who crossed its path. It slammed its tail into the arcades and crashed into the pier. Why was Nova showing him this?

"I was not in charge of the Light Hunters back then," said Nova. "I was a squad leader, just like Ester. My team was sent to Daven. There were four of us. We did our best with what we had, but four Hunters cannot kill a Monster."

More destruction accompanied Nova's words. Lux wanted to look away, but he couldn't. He'd never seen anything of the night his family died, nor of the Cerberus that killed them. He felt fury burning inside him.

"By the time more Hunters got there it was too late."

The scene changed. The Monster was in the town square now, its three heads smashing stone chunks out of the clock-tower. Little flashes of Light lit up the image as the Hunters battled the beast. Lux squinted at a handful of figures on the ground. He recognised Nova, throwing torrents of Light.

"It flattened everything for two miles," said Nova sadly. "I lost two of my team that night, but the town lost so much more – mothers, fathers, sisters, brothers, cousins, aunties, uncles."

Lux stared at the image. He'd come to terms with his family's death long ago, and had always defended the Hunters, despite what other Daven townsfolk said. The Cerberus had attacked and the Hunters had tried to help. It was as simple as that. No-one could blame them. And yet . . . hearing a Hunter claim responsibility for that night reminded Lux of all he'd lost. Would his family still be alive if they hadn't made that mistake?

"We managed to injure the Monster," said Nova. "We slashed one of its eyes – a perfectly vertical slice. But somehow it escaped into the hills. It has not been seen since. But by that point it was too late, anyway." Nova clenched his jaw as a new image appeared on the observatory. This one was dimmer, but clearly from the morning after the attack. Lux could see shattered buildings and shattered people, their faces tired and afraid as they picked desperately through the rubble, searching for loved ones. Most of them were children. Somewhere under the debris were their parents.

"We tried to help with the clean-up, but everyone told us to go. We returned in the weeks that followed, but something had changed. Daven no longer trusted us. They blamed us. In time, they closed our outpost in town and kicked out the Hunters, banning Light completely."

"Who was he?"

Lux's question took Nova by surprise. He lifted his good arm from his robe and scratched his chin. "Excuse me?"

"Your predecessor, the one that made the mistake. It was Deimos, wasn't it?"

Nova sighed heavily. He clicked the controller and a man's face appeared on the dome. His features were familiar to Lux, although he couldn't place them. Where had he seen him before? The face was friendly, with a strong jaw and easy smile. The hair was dark and wavy, but it was the eyes that captivated Lux – soft and deep, like they were looking directly at him. Lux felt like he'd looked into those eyes a thousand times.

And then it hit him.

How could he be such a fool? The reason he felt like he'd stared into those eyes a thousand times was because he had. The man in front of Lux was someone he'd known for as long as he could remember, a figure so important in his life he could hardly believe what he was seeing.

"Is that my..?"

"Yes," said Nova soberly, resting a hand on Lux's shoulder. "The man who made the mistake was your grandpa."

· CHAPTER 29 ·

Lux unhooked himself from Nova's grasp. His grandpa, a fighter of Monsters? An actual Light Hunter? Not just a Hunter, but their Luminary? Could he really be the one that had made the mistake that killed his family.

"He was the best there ever was," said Nova. "He wielded Light like it came from his very soul. But that decision . . ." Nova frowned sadly. "He never got over it."

"But he didn't know, right?" said Lux quickly. "He thought he was sending them all to the right place?"

Nova nodded. "It was still too much. He brooded on it. He had lost his family in the attack. You were all he had left. And as more stories came back from Daven – wrecked families, orphans – we started to lose him. Eventually, he told us all he was leaving. He wanted to look after you and see what he could do to help the rest of town."

Lux gazed at the twinkling stars through the dome. He breathed in and out, trying to control his emotions. How had his grandpa kept this from him? How had he kept it from everybody in Daven?

Lux asked Nova these questions. Nova pointed the controller again. A new image of Daven appeared, one Lux recognised from his childhood. The lighthouse and town square had both been rebuilt.

"Back then, a Light Hunter Luminary spent most of their time at Dawnstar," said Nova. "Nobody in Daven knew what your grandpa looked like, so he was able to enter town as plain old Ben Dowd. He observed the damage, spoke to the townspeople, listened to how they blamed the Light Hunters for the attack. He resolved to assist them in their rebuilding."

Lux closed his eyes. It was a lot to take in.

"Is this why Deimos is after me?" he said miserably. "Because he blames Grandpa for Daven?"

"No. Deimos yearns for more than mere revenge, Lux." The image on the dome changed to depict two figures silhouetted against the burning backdrop of town. The night of the attack. Behind them, the Cerberus's heads thrashed against a church steeple. Lux studied the figures. One was unmistakeably Nova. The other . . .

"You will recall I said two of my team died that night," said Nova. "Deimos was the other survivor."

The second figure turned in the image so his face was visible. Deimos's ashy beard was missing. So, too, was his wide-brimmed hat and overcoat. But in every other way he was the same man Lux had encountered on the beach. Even ten years ago, his face had been lined with crags and pores, his eyes blazing. An anger smouldered inside him, a rage that hunched his shoulders and tensed his jaw.

"Deimos was haunted by that night too. He carried on fighting for the Hunters, but he was different. He spent more time in the library here, reading old texts, learning about the Ancients who came before us. He trained in darker corners of the Light arts – casts we haven't used for centuries. We call it Shade. Deimos became convinced of Shade's power. He tried to persuade the rest of us, claiming it would allow us to battle dozens of Monsters at a time. But Shade is banned in these halls for a reason. Too many have lost themselves to its twisted ways. And one day, after Deimos had tired of trying to change our minds, he just up and vanished."

Lux tried to order things in his mind. Ancients. Deimos. Shade. "But why's he after me now?"

Nova tweaked the image again. This time, it covered the entire dome. A map.

"A year passed and he resurfaced. At first, his appearances were sporadic. Someone saw him while they were out battling Monster spawn. Someone else spotted him scouting Dawnstar. Then our Intelligence team here noticed a pattern." As Nova spoke, red crosses appeared on the map, close to towns and cities. Vileas. Leverburgh. Rothhalt. "Deimos," said Nova bitterly, "was always turning up at a place a week or so before a Monster attack."

Lux recognised the names from assemblies at his school. The Behemoth attack on Vileas. Mr Winter had told them about that. The Amarok attack on Leverburgh. He remembered seeing pictures in books. The Drake assault on Rothhalt.

"We defended these attacks as best we could. After more investigation, we realised Deimos was triggering Monsters to attack towns. Monsters ordinarily act of their own accord, but Deimos had found a way to control them. He was searching for something. We opposed him and became his enemy."

Lux dipped his head. "Wait, you said he wanted to use Shade to *stop* Monster attacks. Why would he attack towns?"

Nova frowned gloomily. "Deimos must consider the damage worth it. To find whatever it is he's looking for."

"But I still don't understand why he needs *me*."

Nova took Lux's hands. "We don't know why Lux, but for some reason you have power in these the likes of which your grandpa had never seen. It has not manifested fully yet, but it will. That's why he taught you, even though he knew it'd get you both in trouble. Someone like you is . . . precious."

Lux pulled away. "I'm not."

Nova crossed to a cabinet and plucked a yellowing piece of paper out of the drawer. He handed it to Lux, who unfolded it. It smelled of his grandpa's workshop – metal and grease.

Artello,

Lux has progressed at a speed I could never have imagined. His power is unique. If what you said in your last letter is true, we cannot let Deimos get his hands on him. You must send someone to get him. I am no longer sure I can protect him.

Sincerely,
Ben Dowd.

"Your grandpa recognised something special in you," said Nova wisely, "and so does Deimos. He wants your power. He believes you can help him. He's been searching for you for a long time. You were in grave danger, back in Daven. Your grandpa, by his quick thinking, saved you."

"What if he didn't save himself?" Lux muttered.

"Excuse me?"

"I said, what if he didn't save himself?"

Nova narrowed his brow. "What do you mean?"

"He's been ill. Grandpa. For months. He was in the house when Deimos was searching for me. What if Deimos got to him?"

Nova eyed Lux and turned away. "Take us down," he called. Lux heard a mechanical hiss and the map on the dome disappeared. Gradually, the platform descended into Nova's room and clicked back into place.

Suddenly, a bark sounded to Lux's left. A dog – a fluffy, furry creature with friendly eyes and floppy ears – leapt at Nova, pawing at his thigh. Nova gathered her up. "Hello Bella, my little girl," he said, shaking his head cheerily. "Shade exerts a terrible force on its user," he said gravely to Lux. "It twists them, makes them capable of unspeakable things. But you underestimate your grandad, Lux. That man has fought demons much larger even than Deimos."

· CHAPTER 30 ·

Nova released Bella and walked to the door. He opened it and a gust of cold air rushed in. Lux shivered.

"Ester!" Nova called out.

"You're to stay with us for now," he said to Lux. "We can guard you from Deimos here. You can join a squad, test your skills. We can teach you things your grandpa couldn't."

Ester appeared in the doorway as Nova spoke. "Lux is going to stay with us. Show him to Squad Juno's dorm. He can be their new Healer."

The compound was silent as Ester led Lux across the moonlit courtyard. He checked his watch. Twelve o' clock. He'd been awake for seventeen hours. Had it really been that long? So much had happened since he'd snuck into the orphanage to see Maya. The thought made him yawn.

Ester giggled at his wide-open mouth.

"He's your dad?" said Lux, still amazed at the idea. "You're Artello Nova's daughter?"

Ester blushed. "For what it's worth, yes."

"I thought you were just a . . ."

"A cleaner?" said Ester. "Then you've learned a valuable lesson." Their footsteps rang loud in the hallway.

"Did he tell you everything?"

"Yes."

"You'll be safe here," said Ester reassuringly. "You can trust us." Lux stopped suddenly. "Where's Maya?"

"She's sleeping." Ester grinned. "You should have seen her. She was out before she'd even got her boots off."

A part of Lux wanted Ester to take him to Maya, but he was too exhausted to ask. Indeed, with each step, Lux grew increasingly tired, his feet dragging behind him.

All his life he'd wrestled to come to terms with being an orphan – losing his mum and dad, his sister. But after his conversation with Nova, everything had changed. His grandpa – a Light Hunter Luminary? Lux just didn't know what to think of that. He didn't know what to think of Deimos or Nova either. He didn't know what to think about Dawnstar or being a Healer. All he knew was that he felt like he was about to collapse.

Lux forced a smile as Ester guided him under an arch and into a long corridor lit by sparkling Light lamps. Dawnstar's dormitories.

Lux saw names above the doors – Salas, Maven, Belex, Celan, more. Ester stopped abruptly at 'Juno,' stamping her heel as if she was in a military parade.

"This is Squad Juno's dorm," she announced, opening the door. "All our Squads are named after stars. You will be with Juno. Your squad-mates are training tonight but they should be back in the morning. Be nice to them, Lux." She fixed him with a hawkish stare that suggested she still remembered all the pranks he played on his classmates at school. Then she kissed his forehead and pushed him into the dorm.

It was quiet inside, with only the sound of a whirring ceiling fan for company. Lux tried to find a lamp but in the end he gave up and lay on one of the beds. Nova had told him he'd be joining a squad. But nobody had even checked with Lux if he wanted to. He understood, of course, that he'd have to stay with the Light Hunters – until they dealt with Deimos, at least. And it was true he and Maya had wanted to *be* Light Hunters for as long as he could remember . . . but those were just playground games. Now he was there, and faced with battling Monsters . . . What if he couldn't heal as well as they thought? What if he wasn't special at all? What if it was all some kind of mistake?

There were three beds in the room, highlighted by thin shafts of moonlight filtering through the blinds. Each was accompanied by a little bedside table. Lux examined them in turn, trying to get a sense of his new squad-mates.

The first bed was unmade, its covers jumbled in a pile on the floor. The table overflowed with objects – wooden games, a pen-knife, a picture frame, a woollen hat and enough bags of sweets to rival *Mrs Miggin's Sugar Rush*. A wooden archer's bow was propped against the bed, and images of Monsters plastered the walls, some with thick black crosses scrawled over them.

The second bed was immaculate, with folded covers and puffed pillows. Items on the side-table were neatly stacked – books, a pencil, a notebook, a glass of water and some wooden Monster figurines. Pieces of paper were tacked to the wall, each filled with small, neat writing.

Lux had never known anyone else his age who could throw Light. He was nervous to meet his squad-mates, but also interested to see what they could do.

He considered this as he struggled sleepily out of his boots and jacket and slid into the remaining bed. Curled up in a ball, his mind drifted to thoughts of his grandpa. A part of Lux was angry at him for keeping secrets. He'd been the only important person in Lux's life for so long. How could he have hidden his past? But Lux also missed his grandpa with a deep, painful ache.

A tear formed in his eye. It remained there as Lux's eyelids drooped and he drifted – slowly – off to sleep.

· CHAPTER 31 ·

Lux woke to a shaft of bright sunlight streaming through an open window. He could hear birds tweeting outside and rustling leaves. He lay in the warmth, his eyes shut, breathing slowly.

His moment of peace was broken by a sharp, commanding voice. "Brace, let him go."

Lux opened his eyes.

The voice belonged to a girl, sat on the neat bed to Lux's left. She was about Lux's age, or perhaps slightly older, with strawberry blonde hair tied in a pigtail to one side, and a big, friendly, moon-shaped face. She held a pencil, and resting on her thighs was the notebook Lux had seen the previous evening. She noticed he was awake and smiled sympathetically.

Lux tried to sit up, but found he was pinned to his bed. He

inspected his feet, where four thin shafts of Light poked out of his trousers, jammed into the mattress. Two more punctured his sleeves. Lux tugged at them. He was trapped.

Why had someone trapped him?

"What kind of a squad-mate would I be if I didn't at least do *some* kind of initiation?" a boy to Lux's right announced.

He was standing by the window, his sun-bleached hair short and spiked, combed back so that he looked a little like a hedgehog. Two buck teeth chomped down in his mouth as he spoke. He wore the same mauve uniform Lux had seen the night before, except his had a line of colourful badges running down the left arm. In his hands, he'd conjured a Light-bow just like the wooden one leaning against his bed. He'd drawn a Light-arrow across it, aimed directly at Lux.

"What's your name anyway, newbie?" he demanded.

Lux tugged again at the Light shafts, but he was locked in. "I'll tell you my name when you let me out of this," he said.

The boy's eyebrows shot up at Lux's response. "Is this kid for real?"

Sliding her pencil irritably into her notebook, the girl swung herself off her bed and padded to Lux.

"I'm sorry about him. It's nothing personal. He does this to all newbies, even when they're not in our squad! I'm Fera Lanceheart III. His name's Braceson James, though most people just call him Brace."

"*Everyone* calls me Brace," corrected the boy.

"What's your name?" asked Fera amiably.

"L-Lux."

Fera started to remove the Light shafts from Lux's clothing, tossing them over her shoulder where they dissipated in the morning breeze. As soon as Brace realised what she was doing, he dismissed his Light-bow and leapt forwards. He'd made it less than a yard when a wall of hovering blue spikes appeared in front of him, their razor-sharp blades pointing at his teeth.

"If you take another step," said Fera calmly, "your face is going to look like a cheese grater."

Brace stopped, his cheeks red with frustration. He tried to sidestep the spikes but they followed him around. He balled his fists and punched the air in frustration.

"So, Lux," said Fera cheerfully, "you're the newest member of Squad Juno. Lucky you. I suppose that means you're a Healer?"

Fera had plucked out the last of the Light arrows. She stepped back as Lux sat up. He studied his torn clothes. "Yes, I'm a Healer."

"Well, I'm a Conjuror. Queen of destruction. *Ice, Bolt, Flame*; you name it, I can do it." Fera pirouetted, issuing a web of Light from her fingers. "This numbskull," she said, dismissing her wall of spikes, "is an Archer. Hence the bow. He's also an idiot, but I'm sure you've worked that one out for yourself."

Lux chuckled. Brace seemed unsure at first how to react. Then he put a protective arm around Fera and squeezed firmly. "Well, someone's got to look after you," he said. "We can't have newbies walking around here until I've vetted them."

Newbie? thought Lux. *Vetted?*

Fera extracted herself from Brace's grip and eyed him

exasperatedly. She retrieved her notebook and began to draw again. Lux faced Brace, who stood with his hands on his hips, appraising him. He shot out a hand.

"You know what, Lux? You seem all right. You haven't put a wall of spikes in front of my face, at least, which is more than I can say for *some* people around here."

On her bed, Fera pumped a clawed shape with her fingers and thumb. "Blah blah blah."

Lux slumped down. This wasn't quite how he'd expected to meet his new squad-mates. "I've never met any other kids who could throw Light."

"Neither had I before I came here," said Brace, retrieving his wooden bow and setting it to his shoulder. "I thought I was the only one."

"Well, you are pretty unique," joked Fera.

"Where are you from anyway?" asked Brace. "Normally they tell us when there's someone new coming."

Lux rubbed his eyes. "I'm from Daven."

"Daven?" Brace pursed his lips, thinking. "So, that was . . . the Cerberus attack ten years ago."

Lux was impressed. He knew a bit about Light Hunters history, but even *he* couldn't name the last Monster to attack a place just like that.

"Don't worry," assured Fera heartily, "Brace has an encyclopaedic knowledge of Monster attacks. He could tell you every major Monster attack in every town going back two-hundred years."

"It's all up here, baby," said Brace, tapping his temple. "I'm from Triev, by the way. The Light Hunters picked me up when I was ten."

"How old are you now?" said Lux.

"I'm fourteen. Fera's thirteen. She's from one of the richest families in Lindhelm."

Fera slammed her notepad onto her thighs. "Brace!"

"What?" He shrugged innocently. "Lux here's our new squadmate. He'll find out sooner or later."

Fera looked embarrassed. "It's true. I am a Lindhelm Lanceheart. But that doesn't mean anything. I'm here because I'm good with Light."

Brace agreed. "She is pretty good."

"How good are you?" Fera asked Lux curiously. "The last Healer we had was awful. We could really do with someone decent."

It was a hard question to answer. Truthfully, Lux had no idea how good he was at throwing Light.

"Well," Fera prodded helpfully, "do you know *Heal? Protect?*" Lux nodded as she recited the casts. Fera tilted her head and stared. "You know them all already?"

"Yes." Lux rose from his bed and walked to the open window. Fera and Brace shared a surprised glance.

"Without any training?" probed Brace dubiously.

"My grandpa taught me."

"Your grandpa . . ." Fera and Brace spoke simultaneously. Lux flushed. Had he said too much? Nova hadn't mentioned whether to reveal what was happening with Deimos. Lux figured it better to be cautious. He searched the room for a distraction and found one in Fera's notes.

"I like these," he said, pointing at the display. "What are they?"

"They're all plans," she said, re-attaching a hand-drawn note that had slid off the wall, "for our squad. To be a good Hunter, you've got to plan, think about your positioning."

Lux surveyed the images – kaleidoscopes of dots, lines and arrows. A sudden realisation hit him that he had absolutely no idea what it meant to be a Light Hunter. He'd learned about devastating Monster attacks and famous Hunters from his sister's books. But he'd never learned what a squad was. He didn't know anything about how a Conjuror fights with an Archer, or how a Healer supports them. He had no idea how Light Hunters trained, how many were sent to Monster attacks, anything . . .

"So, we're going to be teammates?" said Lux. "We'll be working together?"

"You really don't know much about this, do you?" said Fera sympathetically.

"Not really. I only got here last night."

"That's all right. Get changed into your uniform and we'll give you a tour."

Brace was already behind Lux with a fresh outfit. He and Fera looked out of the window as Lux changed. When he was done, he coughed.

"You look good, man," said Brace enthusiastically.

"Yes, nice," agreed Fera.

Lux found a mirror in the wardrobe. The mauve uniform was

immaculate – made from a soft material. He twisted around, trying to see it from all angles. On his right arm was a circular badge, adorned with a green cross. Healing. He peered over at Fera and Brace, who each sported a symbol of their own alongside a line of Monster badges – Fera a yellow lightning bolt and Brace a blue bow.

Brace caught Lux staring at his Monster badges. "You get them when you kill a Monster," he explained. "One for each."

"Nice."

Brace bowed theatrically and then clicked his fingers, impatient to leave. "Should we wait for number four?"

"Number four?" repeated Lux, thinking immediately of Maya.

"Oh my, they didn't tell you anything at *all*, did they?" Fera slapped a palm to her forehead. "Every squad has four members. Three kids and a leader. The leader's always a more experienced Hunter."

"Where's ours?" asked Lux.

"Right here."

Leaning against the door, her Gauntlet repaired and an amused grin on her face, was Ester Hart.

· CHAPTER 32 ·

"Welcome to my squad, Lux."

"You're Squad Juno's leader?" said Lux incredulously. "Why didn't you say?"

"You didn't ask."

Brace stepped between Lux and Ester. "Wait, you two know each other?"

"It was my job to bring him here," said Ester.

Brace stood still, digesting the news. He clapped Lux on the shoulder. "Wow!" he said, smiling at Fera. "He really must be something to have the boss's daughter as a chaperone!"

Fera inclined her head in agreement. Ester entered the room. Her eyebrows shot up when she saw the holes in Lux's bedsheets. She looked questioningly between Brace and Fera. "Care to explain?"

Lux's heart skipped a beat. Brace pleaded silently for him to keep quiet.

"It was an . . . accident," said Lux uncertainly. He poked a finger into one of the holes. "Brace was showing me what an Archer does and he hit my bed."

Ester frowned sceptically. "With four arrows?"

Lux nodded.

"In a perfect square?"

Brace skipped forward. "You *know* I'm good."

Ester dismissed the topic. "Listen, we don't have time for this. I have orders from Nova. He wants you two to show Lux around Dawnstar. Explain how things work."

"Already on our way," said Fera.

"Good, I'm glad someone around here has a brain. Make sure you pick up Maya on the way. She's in Squad Celan's room."

"Maya?" echoed Brace, puzzled.

"Lux will explain."

With that, Ester nodded a farewell and disappeared. Brace leapt in front of Lux and pumped his hand.

"Thanks for that. I owe you one."

"You owe both of us," said Fera sternly. "Now," she said, turning to Lux, "who's this Maya?"

Lux explained how he knew Maya, and also how she'd ended up at Dawnstar with him and Ester.

"But she can't use Light?" checked Brace.

"No."

"And she's here?"

"Somewhere."

"Lucky girl," said Brace, shaking his head.

"Some would say *you're* lucky to be here even though you *can* use Light," Fera shot at Brace. "Now, stop being irritating and let's go show Lux the sights."

Their tour started in the dormitories, where four wings ran off a central spine.

"Each squad has their own room," Fera explained, peeking into an open door and waving at a pair of young Hunters inside. "You'll have a Tech like Ester. You know they can't personally manipulate Light, yes? They use Gauntlets. And you'll have at least one Healer and two offensive Hunters. Any class can be a leader, but more often than not they're the oldest."

Lux poked his head into the room. It had a similar layout to Squad Juno's, with three beds and bedside tables. He waved to the occupants and they waved back.

Soon, they reached a room marked 'Celan.' Inside, Maya was sitting on a bed, looking thoroughly bored.

"There you are!" she said, relieved. "I was worried. Ester said you'd be coming." Maya peered beyond Lux at Fera and Brace. "Who are they?"

Lux scooted aside so his new squad-mates could enter. Brace dropped theatrically to a knee in front of Maya and extended a hand just like a knight greeting his princess. "Pleasure to meet you."

Maya looked down at Brace, unsure of how to react. "Okay . . ."

"As I said to Lux earlier," said Fera, shunting Brace aside and extending a hand for Maya, "ignore him. I'm Fera. Nice to meet you."

"Nice to meet you too."

Lux updated Maya on all that had happened. He considered telling her what Nova had said about Deimos and his grandpa. And if they'd been on their own, he might well have done. But something told Lux he should keep that a secret from Brace and Fera. For now, at least.

Lux told Maya about their tour around Dawnstar. She nearly popped with excitement. "We're going to see all of it?"

"The bits we can show you," said Fera, chuckling at Maya's enthusiasm.

Brace led them all to the elevators, where they descended two levels and made their way along a narrow passage bathed in green Light.

"This," he said eagerly, bursting through a pair of double doors, "is our training wing."

They'd arrived at a viewing gallery in a cavernous room. Lux could see a jungle of platforms, Light-traps, tunnels, climbing frames, targets, hanging ropes, holograms and training Monsters – all intersecting each other so that he found it hard to tell where one ended and another began.

"Cool, don't you think?" said Brace, sticking up an excited thumb.

"It's so big!" said Maya, leaning over the edge.

"Most older Hunters spend their time doing recon in the field or in here training new recruits," said Fera. "There aren't as many young Hunters as there used to be but there're still a few of us left." She drew herself upright, proud.

Fera and Brace stood back as Lux and Maya watched a procession of young Hunters being drilled by an older Light Hunter with an eyepatch. Lux focussed on one kid in particular – a short, stocky boy with curly hair and an eagle nose – who ran, jumped, shot Light arrows, ducked, stabbed, crawled and swung – all in the space of a minute. It was – quite simply – the most exciting thing Lux had ever seen.

"Will I get to do that?" he asked Fera.

"Most of it."

Lux shook his head, amazed.

"Don't get too excited. You'll be wishing you'd never set foot in the place after a week. Come on, there's lots more to see."

Lux and Maya dragged themselves away and followed Fera and Brace into the atrium. There, they threaded their way through passages thick with Hunters and walls covered with Monster diagrams. At the end of a particularly narrow corridor, Lux spied another set of double doors with 'Intelligence' written in gold lettering. Brace held him back.

"We can't go in there. Squad leaders only."

"Why's that?" asked Lux, curious.

Brace made air quotes and adopted an authoritative voice uncannily similar to Artello Nova's. "Sensitive information."

Fera took them down an adjoining corridor and up a steep flight of stairs into the skyship hangar. It had been empty the previous night when Lux and Maya passed through. Now, the place bustled with activity. Light-bridges criss-crossed the space, allowing pilots and engineers to travel easily between docked skyships. Lux could see at least a dozen crafts – huge, hulking, metal contraptions with crackling Light-engines. He squinted up at the roof, which was punctured with gaps wide enough for skyships to fit through. One was descending now, loudly motoring to an empty docking space.

"I'm going to drive a skyship one day," said Brace resolutely, miming controlling one with his hands.

"If you don't drive us all wappy first," said Fera.

They watched engineers stumble under the weight of giant toolboxes as they lugged them between ships. Lux could hardly believe all this had been happening near Daven and nobody had known a thing.

"All right," said Fera, when they'd had enough, "time to go see the workshops."

But before she could move, a loud boom sounded somewhere in the distance. The walkway shuddered violently, shunting Lux into the rail. Loose parts and tools vibrated off ships as rubble rained in from above. Had a skyship crashed in the crater? Lux wondered. Or was it Deimos? Surely he couldn't be at Dawnstar? Up on the Light-bridges, the engineers all exchanged nervous glances. Fera and Brace joined them. Only when they saw a cloud of grey-black smoke rolling quickly down the corridor did they understand. A single word passed their lips.

"Tesla!"

· CHAPTER 33 ·

Fera and Brace sprinted down the walkway to the stairs. Before Lux could follow, Maya gripped his forearm.

"They said Tesla, right?"

"Yes."

Maya rocked on her heels in excitement.

They caught up with Fera and Brace at the bottom of the staircase. A door opened and in stepped two older Hunters.

"Where is he?" asked Fera anxiously.

One of the Hunters jerked a thumb over his shoulder.

Fera motored down the passage, weaving left and right as Lux, Brace and Maya followed. At the atrium, she catapulted over the guard rail, landing neatly on the level below. Lux skidded to a halt when he realised he'd have to follow. Maya took the chance to push ahead, swinging herself over as easy as if she was jumping the groynes back on Daven beach. Determined not to be outdone, Lux backed up, counted to three and darted towards the rail. He twisted over the top, letting out a high-pitched yelp as he plummeted. He landed with a *thud* on the floor below.

"Stylish," teased Maya, helping him up.

Hunters rushed out of the elevators carrying full buckets of water, while others travelled in the opposite direction, their faces soot-blackened. Fera, Brace, Lux and Maya followed those with the buckets, until the corridor was shrouded in smoke. From somewhere amongst the grey veil, they heard an impatient, cackling voice.

"All right, all right, we've all seen a fifteen-ton Light explosion before. Don't get excited." A man in a wheelchair appeared out of the mist. He had shoulder-length, salt-and-pepper dreadlocks. "Go and do some real work. Nova ain't paying you to have a water fight!" Fera and Brace wafted the smoke and approached him.

"Well, if it ain't Zippy and Dippy," he said tersely. "Remind me next time I need assistance to ask a couple of turnips instead."

"What happened?" asked Brace.

"We learned that one man isn't enough to test a new Light-cast. Even if he is a super-genius like me." As he spoke, the man pointed to his wheelchair and gestured for Fera to wheel him inside. "Now, make yourselves useful and help me tidy up."

Maya leaned closer to Lux. "That's him, isn't it?"

"Tesla? Looks like it."

Maya darted after Fera, leaving Brace and Lux in the corridor. Brace looked confused.

"She's obsessed with tech," Lux explained. "He's sort of her hero."

Brace looked baffled. "Tesla? Funny hero."

Tesla's laboratory was about the size of Lux's grandpa's workshop. A symphony of noises was playing – hums, clicks, puffs of steam. Benches filled the space, running like snakes across the room. Every inch of wood was covered – Light-blades, crossbows, broken Gauntlets, books, clocks, lanterns, lab-coats, more. There was a large glass chamber in one corner, inside of which levitated a metal bar. Smoke billowed from the metal, drifting lazily to the ceiling.

Fera wheeled Tesla through the mess. "So . . .?" he said questioningly.

"So . . .?"

"Where were you?"

Tesla was an older man, Lux could see – thin, with long, wiry muscles and a big, toothy mouth. His jaw veered off to one side as if it had been cracked and never put back. Lux wondered if it hurt.

"I'm so sorry," said Fera guiltily. "I totally forgot."

"You forgot? You forgot to be here for the demonstration of the first new cast in fifteen years? You forgot?" Tesla threw up his hands, exasperated. He wheeled himself to the glass chamber and worked at tightening a screw there. "Who are they?" he demanded brusquely.

"This is Lux and Maya," said Brace.

Tesla eyed Maya shrewdly. "I've not heard your name," he said, before turning to Lux, "but you're the one Deimos is after."

"I . . . I don't know about any of that," said Brace, puzzled, "but he's our new squad-mate."

"Poor lad."

"Hey!" objected Fera. "Squad Juno is good."

"Yes, very good. At being *late*!"

There was a loud bark behind one of the counters. Nova's dog, Bella, barrelled out of the smoke. She pulled up, shook her sandy fur and wandered up to Tesla, who stroked her fondly.

"A year I've been working on this, and it's failed," he grumbled.

"Surely you can just run it again?" blurted Maya, before she could stop herself.

Tesla fixed her with a withering stare. "Of *course* I can run it again, but that's not my point. My point is, if I ask someone to be here at ten," he indicated Fera and Brace, "I want them here at ten. Those two are about as useful as an ice-cream fireplace."

Tesla returned to his work. Lux, Fera and Brace exchanged a glance.

"I can see you staring!"

Lux picked at the objects on the counter, lifting a book and plucking a crossbow string. *I'd quite like a go with this,* he thought, as he enjoyed the satisfying *twang.* A clay model of a Monster stood in one corner, next to an old map on the wall. Lux ran his hand along the creature's spiked tail and squat, rough body.

" . . .they told you who I am?"

Lux heard the words but didn't realise Tesla was addressing him. "Sorry?" he said, spinning around.

Tesla wheeled away from the chamber and repeated himself, slowly and clearly. "Have. They. Told. You. Who. I. Am?"

"*I* know who you are," said Maya excitedly, jumping between them. "You're Tesla. Inventor. Head of Light Hunter technology. Smartest graduate ever from Lindhelm University and quickest Hunter ever through the Dawnstar initiation test. I've read every book you've ever written."

Tesla arched his eyebrows. "Poor, poor girl." He turned to Lux again. "Anyway, young man, you're going to get to know me *very* well." He sorted through a pile of boxes and pulled out an apple, taking a bite. "Your friend is right, I am the brains of this place. The Inventor. I test casts and make the gadgets, Gauntlets, engines and who knows what else."

"The explosions?" said Lux.

Tesla stopped eating. All the hairs on the back of Lux's neck stood on end. But a devilish smile broke across the Inventor's face. "I like these two," he said. "What did you say their names were?"

Lux stepped forward before Fera could answer. "Lux and Maya."

"Lux and Maya, eh?" The old man tested their names on his tongue. "Well, kiddos, settle in because I've got a little story to tell you."

· CHAPTER 34 ·

Tesla wheeled to a counter and took out an old, faded child's doll from a drawer. He handed it to Lux.

"That toy belonged to a young girl," he said, reclining in his wheelchair. "Her father contacted the Light Hunters asking us to escort her across Snake Pass Valley so she could start a new life with her aunt in Lindhelm. This was a few years back."

Lux turned the doll over in his hand. Its clothes were frayed.

"I was a young Light Hunter at the time. It was my third mission, and the first Nova had trusted me to undertake alone. Have you heard of Snake Pass Valley?"

Lux had a think. He was sure Mr Garside had mentioned it in one of their Geography lessons, but he couldn't remember anything specific.

"It runs between the Shengan Jungle and Lindhelm. It's a dangerous place, even for a Light Hunter."

Lux put the doll down and gave Tesla his full attention.

"We'd made it halfway along the pass without seeing a single Monster when suddenly we were set upon by a beast." Tesla sat up in his chair and wheeled to the Monster statue Lux had seen earlier. "I got the girl onto a ledge, then I went at the Monster with everything I had. But I was no match. It forced me up against a cliff and . . ." Tesla trailed off. He looked sadly at the empty fabric below his waist.

"The Monster took the girl. Nova sent a team to find us. Miraculously, I survived. The girl wasn't so lucky."

Silence filled the laboratory. Tesla's eyes rested on the map on the wall.

"They could have replaced my limbs with Light ones," he gestured to a rack of mechanical limbs behind the glass chamber, "but I declined. The girl had lost her life. It only seemed right I lose something too."

Fera put a hand on Tesla's shoulder.

"I've worked as Dawnstar's Inventor ever since."

Lux walked to the map and fingered some of the pins. To the north, he could see the sprawl of Lindhelm, its name printed in elaborate script. To the south was the Shengan Jungle.

"Sightings," explained Tesla, joining Lux and pushing in a loose pin. "It's a rare beast. A Behemoth. No more than five in the world. Each pin represents a sighting in the valley." He paused. "Since we lost the little girl."

"So why hasn't it been killed?" asked Maya.

Tesla looked at Fera and Brace, then at Maya.

"This is a personal endeavour," he said stiffly. He brushed his dreadlocks from his face. "Nobody goes to Snake Pass any more. Nova doesn't want to assign any resources to it. So, it's my job to kill this thing." His eyes rested on the glass blast chamber.

"And that's going to be the cast to do it," said Lux, understanding at last why Tesla was telling them his story.

"They really are quick, these two," Tesla said to Fera and Brace. He wheeled to a counter buried under a mountain of papers – sketches, notes, reports – and lifted each, showing them briefly to Lux and Maya. "Seven years I've been working on this cast. Seven, long years I've spent figuring it out and at last I'm close. If we can control this *Blast*, I think I'll be able and finish this thing, *wherever* it is."

Lux studied the ceiling where a few last wisps of smoke were escaping out of the window. "So that's what caused the . . ."

"Explosion, yes," said Tesla roughly.

"What went wrong?" asked Fera, pushing herself off the bench.

Tesla put down his notes and smiled sweetly at her. "That's an easy one. I must have jigged the scombulator to kick in when the Light whizzimigig shut off."

"Really?" Lux cocked his head, impressed. He'd never heard of any of those things.

"No!" said Tesla, screwing up his face in irritation. "They're not even real words. What *is* real," he said grouchily, jabbing a finger at Fera and Brace, "is the incompetence of these two, who left me high and dry. I nearly blasted my face off!"

Fera and Brace blushed.

"So, can't you just try it again?" said Lux simply.

Tesla rolled his eyes. He retrieved his spanner and screwed at a mechanical gadget in his lap. "I already have."

"You've already . . .?" Brace trailed off. "You've already reset it?"

Tesla looked up. "Of course."

"When?" said Fera.

"A few minutes ago."

Lux thought of the enormous explosion he'd felt back in the sky-ship hangar and the wall of grey smoke that had blocked their path.

Tesla caught their anxious stares. "Oh," he said, suddenly understanding, "you're worried about yourselves? Do you really think I'm that stupid?"

Lux and Fera glanced at the door.

"Oh for goodness sake," said Tesla, throwing up his hands in exasperation, "I wasn't born yesterday. The *Blast's* locked in now. There's nothing to worry about."

Lux breathed a sigh of relief. Tesla was *the* Light Hunter Inventor; he obviously knew what he was doing.

Inside the chamber, hazy, blue-white Light surrounded the black metal bar. It expanded slowly – little electric tendrils tracing swirling patterns on the glass. Lux reached out to touch them and froze. At the bottom of the chamber, obscured by the Light, was a dark furry shape. Lux bent down to get a closer look. What he found made him gasp.

Cowering at the bottom of the chamber, a look of intense fear in her hazel-brown eyes, was Artello Nova's dog, Bella.

· CHAPTER 35 ·

Fera leapt forward and slammed a palm into the glass. Bella jumped up and barked excitedly, wagging her tail. "Tell me you can get her out."

"It's ah . . ." Tesla paused. "That's not going to be easy."

"Just open the chamber!" shouted Brace frantically.

Tesla grimaced. "I can't, not when the cast's started."

"You're kidding?"

Tesla wheeled towards the glass chamber, shaking his head. "Systems like this, once they're in motion . . ."

"There must be an off button," said Lux. There had to be one. He leaned around Tesla's chair to see the control panel.

"Can you stop a cast partway through?" asked Tesla waspishly.

Lux thought about it. He couldn't. It was one of the first things his grandpa had taught him – don't start a cast unless you're absolutely sure you want to go through with it. A quick look at Fera and Brace told Lux they were the same.

Tesla hammered the control panel, trying to get it to respond. It emitted a high-pitched drone as the Light in the chamber expanded. Bella shivered.

"How did she get in there?" asked Maya as Brace rammed a shoulder into the chamber, trying to get it open. Lux helped him.

"I don't know," snapped Tesla. "Perhaps if you two had been here when . . ."

"Enough!" Fera's shout silenced them all. "How long does she have?"

Tesla checked an egg-timer on his desk. Most of the sand had fallen. "A minute. Maybe less."

Lux's heart jumped. There had to be some way to get her out. He shoved his body into the chamber again, groaning with the effort. Tesla slammed his wrench into the glass until his cheeks turned red and beads of sweat fell off his forehead. Nothing. He stared at Bella. Her eyes drooped sadly.

Lux and the others pulled away, their cheeks pale. Only Fera stayed, pressing her nose up against the glass. The egg-timer passed its final grains.

A noise rocked the chamber – excruciatingly loud. Jars and beakers rattled in their cupboards. Gadgets smashed on the ground. The blast shunted Lux to his right. He thrust his hands to his ears, closing his eyes. Brace and Maya joined him, doubling over. The rumblings and crashes came to an abrupt stop. Then there was an explosion of Light – so bright Lux could see it through his eyelids. It waxed and waned, flashed one last time and died.

Nobody moved. One by one, they turned around. The entire room was blanketed in smoke. Lux pulled his shirt to his mouth and wafted with his free hand. Tesla hunched over in his chair, lips pressed together.

In the chamber, the Light had shrunk to the size of a pea, firing static threads at the glass panels. Lux looked at the base and frowned. Bella lay still, her tail wrapped around her body and mouth slack.

Fera burst into tears. Brace wrapped an arm around her, appealing to Lux, Maya and Tesla for help. He settled on Lux, who struggled at first to work out what Brace wanted. Then he understood.

He was a Healer.

Brace wanted him to do something.

The floor disappeared beneath Lux. He tasted panic in his mouth. It was true, he *was* a Healer. He could fix injuries. He'd done that for his grandpa dozens of times when he'd cut himself in the workshop. But he couldn't bring things back from the dead. He paced nervously.

"There's nothing I can do now," he said feebly.

"Try something," snapped Brace.

"I can't!"

"What's going on?" asked Tesla.

"He's a Healer," said Brace.

Tesla looked between Brace and Lux. He tilted his head

towards the older boy, a look of admonishment on his face. "Now, hang on . . ."

He stopped.

Tesla closed his eyes and tapped his temple. He propelled his chair past Lux to a bookshelf on the other side of the room, flipping over another, smaller egg-timer as he went. Running a finger along the spines, he muttered their titles. He stopped at a blue, leather book and placed it on his lap.

"Is he right?" he asked Lux sharply. "Are you a Healer?"

"I can heal, but . . ."

"What's going on?" asked Maya curiously. She tried to get a look at the book's title.

Tesla rifled through it until he found what he was looking for and jabbed a finger at the page.

"There's a very old healing cast called *Revive*," he explained. "Very old. No-one's been able to cast it for decades."

Lux examined the page. Most of it was covered with faded ink – long tables of dates and numbers. But the section Tesla had indicated was different. Instead of a table, the word *Revive* was written in old, cursive text next to an image of a Light cast. Lux recognised the layout from books his grandpa kept at the workshop. Instructions for how to throw a cast. He backed away.

"You want me to throw this?"

"No-one else can," said Tesla.

"But I've never seen it before."

"I know." Tesla glanced at the hourglass.

"What if I get it all wrong?" said Lux, panicking.

Tesla didn't answer.

"What makes you even think I can do it?"

"I don't," admitted Tesla honestly. He gestured at Bella, and Fera sobbing beside her. "But it's worth a shot."

Lux looked at Fera and the dog, regretting his decision even as he made it. "Okay," he said, "I'll give it a go."

· CHAPTER 36 ·

Tesla clapped his hands. But his expression changed quickly to a grimace.

"There's just one problem." He placed the small egg-timer on the bench. "*Revive* has a time-limit."

Lux frowned. "A time-limit?"

"A short one. About four minutes and forty-six seconds."

Lux frowned, confused. How could a cast have a time-limit? None he'd ever thrown had a time-limit.

"Are you saying it takes four minutes to cast?"

"No," said Tesla, "you've got four minutes to *throw* it. After that, it's too late."

Lux looked at the timer. "How long do we have left?"

"Three minutes."

Lux ground his teeth. He flicked a hand towards the chamber. "Go on then. I'm guessing this won't pass through glass."

Tesla turned a series of dials on the chamber control panel. The glass panes hissed and unlatched. Brace darted forward to catch the first and hauled it aside. Meanwhile, Lux pored over Tesla's book, trying to memorise the cast. He found a space in the middle of the room and practised the motions. Sparks of Light swirled around him, ricocheting off counters.

Brace retrieved Bella and lay her on a blanket by Lux. Tesla wheeled over, the egg-timer in his lap. Half the sand was gone.

Lux examined Bella – her nose still glistening – and started the cast. *Just get it right,* he thought. Branches of blue-white Light crawled from his hands, swirling around him. He tensed his forearms, trying to control them. Then he drew the Light in, so that a half-moon of energy formed between his fingers. Lux checked the egg-timer – a quarter left – and closed his eyes. *Come on, come on.* The crescent was humming now, and he tensed his arms once more, forcing one last blast of energy into the Light. Then he flicked his fingers towards Bella. The Light enveloped her, turning her skin blue. The others leaned in as the Light rippled, not daring to breathe.

"Well?" said Fera impatiently.

Maya stooped so her ear was level with Bella's muzzle. She shook her head.

Fera turned away. Lux caught Tesla's eye.

"Again," he ordered.

Lux grimaced. This time, he formed the half-moon in seconds.

Better, he thought. He breathed, channelling more and more energy into the cast. Soon, the Light stung his hands, but he held on. *Just a few more seconds.* Then he let go. The half-moon of energy lit up Bella like a candle, so forceful it made her twitch. Lux and Brace winced, but it stopped almost as soon as it had started. The Light faded.

Maya pressed her ear to Bella's muzzle and listened. Fera waited, her face wet with tears. "Yes?"

Maya dipped her eyes. "Sorry." The last grains of sand squeezed through the timer. Lux felt a sharp pain in his chest.

They stayed like this, nobody speaking.

It was Brace who broke the silence, gathering up Bella and wrapping her gently in the blanket.

"I guess I'd better go and tell Nova," said Tesla sadly. He accepted Bella on his lap. "She was a good dog."

Fera and Brace nodded.

Tesla rolled towards Lux. "Good try, kid. You did better than most."

Yeah, but not good enough, thought Lux miserably.

Tesla wheeled towards the door. As he did, there was a movement in his lap. Lux checked whether Brace and Fera had noticed it too, but they were locked in a hug. Puzzled, he watched the blanket closely. Another twitch. Tesla noticed it this time. Lux heard a whimper under the fabric.

"Bella!"

A brown mass of fur and slobber exploded from Tesla's lap, landing in front of his wheelchair. Bella scratched an ear and scrambled across to Fera, leaping up and pawing at her stomach. The five humans shared a glance and burst into a storm of cheering and wooping and high-fiving. Brace barrelled into Lux, bouncing him into Tesla's Monster statue and sending it tumbling.

"I don't believe it!" He grinned.

Tesla shook his head in amazement. He held out a hand to Lux. "You're the first person in decades who's pulled that off."

"I don't think that's the last thing he's going to do," said Fera, gathering up Bella and cradling her in her arms.

"Incredible," said Tesla.

"He sure is," said Brace excitedly. He crushed Lux in a bear-hug. "Squad Juno's going right to the top!"

Lux grinned. He'd done it. He wasn't quite sure *how* he'd done it, but somehow he had.

· CHAPTER 37 ·

Tesla spent a while running Bella through a bunch of tests to check she was all right. Bella undertook them patiently, wagging her tail and barking every time she saw Fera. After the seventh examination, Tesla presented her with a slice of ham, declaring her one hundred percent healthy.

"Well, all's well that ends well," he said cheerfully, rubbing his hands together. "Bella's all right, the *Blast* worked and everyone's still alive."

Fera fixed Tesla with an exasperated stare.

"Though perhaps it *might* be worth keeping this amongst ourselves," added Tesla, shrugging innocently. "I don't think there's any need to worry an important man like Artello Nova with rumours of his dog being brought back to life. Agreed?"

Without waiting for their response, Tesla began to shoo them out of his lab, muttering about cleaning up and running his experiment again. "Got to replicate the data. Got to replicate the data."

At the door, Lux turned to give Bella a last grin. He was surprised to see that Maya hadn't moved. "Maya?"

She grimaced.

Lux understood immediately. He walked back inside. "Tesla," he said, "I think Maya wants to stay."

Tesla put the egg-timer he'd been tidying away onto a shelf. "That's not up to me. You'll have to speak to Nova."

"No," said Lux. "She wants to stay *here*. With you. You're . . ." He grasped for the right words, ". . . you're sort of her hero. She's a techie." Lux regarded Maya, whose cheeks were turning crimson. "In fact, she's pretty incredible at it. Do you think she could stay for a bit, help you out?"

Tesla turned around. "Absolutely not! I don't have time to be babysitting every stray that wanders in."

"She repaired Ester's Gauntlet."

Tesla paused at this. He seemed to think, then retrieved the device's charred remains from his desk. "So, it was you who fiddled with my creation?"

Maya winced.

"Pretty good work, that was."

"It was easy," said Maya, shrugging.

Tesla smirked. He thought again as he wheeled his chair back to the cupboard with the timers.

"It's a first, but I'm actually going to let you stay. For a while, at least. But don't get in my way." He twisted in his seat and thrust up a warning forefinger. "And you must do everything I say, as soon as I say it. Is that clear?"

Maya nodded eagerly.

Tesla spread his palms. "Well," he said impatiently, "what are you waiting for? That *Blast* chamber won't reassemble itself."

Maya jerked in excitement.

"Be good, all right?" said Lux, smiling.

Maya skipped towards the glass panels.

Lux exited the lab and found Brace and Fera out in the corridor. Brace had conjured a ball of Light and was bouncing it idly in his hands while Fera had slumped to the ground, bored. When she saw Lux, she jumped up.

"What?" said Lux.

"Just . . . *that*," said Fera, "Since I've been at Dawnstar, probably twenty kids have asked Tesla if they can work with him. He's said no to all of them."

Lux shrugged. "There's more to Maya than meets the eye."

For the rest of the day, Fera and Brace continued Lux's tour around Dawnstar, poking their heads into every nook and cranny. Medical bays, gyms, libraries, gardens, recreation rooms, more. By the time they'd finished, it was approaching dinnertime. They trudged into the dining hall behind a stream of younger Hunters, fresh from training. Lux was starving. He loaded his plate with chicken, vegetables and chips and staggered back to their table.

"I have never been so hungry in my life!" he said, shoving a chip into his mouth. It was hot and crispy and tasted amazing.

Fera told them she'd be back shortly and left their table. Brace scooted around so he was sitting beside Lux.

"Thanks for this morning," he said quietly.

"For what?"

"Bella. Fera would kill me if she knew I was telling you this, but . . . she had a dog when she was little. It ran off when they were walking at the back of her estate. Some Monster spawn got it. Wouldn't have been good if we'd lost Bella too."

When Fera came back, she noticed Lux and Brace staring.

"What?" she asked, checking she hadn't spilled dinner on her uniform.

"Nothing," said Brace stiffly.

Fera regarded them sceptically, then rolled her eyes and shook her head. Brace winked at Lux.

Soon, a crowd of younger Hunters approached Lux from another table.

"We heard about Tesla's lab," said one breathlessly. "Amazing!"

"*Revive*," said another. "I can't believe it."

"You should come and heal for Squad Maven," said a ginger-haired girl with freckles. "Don't waste your time with these losers." She winked playfully at Fera and Brace, grabbed a chair from a neighbouring table and sat down.

Lux proceeded to answer a hundred-and-one questions. Where was he born? When did he realise he could throw Light? Who taught him? Had he ever got into trouble for it? What was it like living somewhere where everybody hated Light? Had he ever been caught using it? Where did he go to school? What did he think of Dawnstar? Was he looking forward to training? Had he fought any Monsters? And on and on and on . . .

Lux answered as best he could, making something up if he thought Nova wouldn't want him to tell the truth. But it had been a long couple of days, and soon he grew so confused from trying to keep all his answers straight in his head that he waited for the other Hunters to start talking amongst themselves, thanked Fera and Brace and then slipped out of the dining hall.

· CHAPTER 38 ·

Lux felt like a rubber band stretched too far. He walked down the corridor, eyes on the floor.

Back in Daven, when he felt down, he would walk on the beach, or visit the memorial garden and speak to his parents and his sister. But in Dawnstar, there was no ocean, or garden, or workshop, or *Mrs Miggin's Sugar Rush,* or any of the places that anchored Lux to his life.

He thought about finding Maya, but he knew she'd be excited after her day with Tesla and Lux wasn't quite in the mood for that. Instead, he navigated to the main atrium and rode an elevator down to the ground floor. Approaching the entrance, he sidestepped through to the platform with the star-shaped lock. Aware that he couldn't get back inside without Ester's ring, he wedged the door open with a heavy stone and sat with his legs dangling over the edge.

It was a cloudless night and all the stars hung like little white pins. It smelled fresh and earthy, like it had just rained. Lux looked at the cluster of trees that marked the hidden sandstone tunnel back to the valley. He sighed. He loved what he'd experienced of Dawnstar – the Light Hunters, Nova, Tesla, Fera, Brace – but with Deimos hunting him, and no word from his grandpa, it was all too much. He was only a kid. He wasn't old enough to be dealing with all this stuff yet. Special? A talent nobody else had? A part of Lux wanted to escape, to run all the way home. He wanted things to be as they were before. He bunched his fist and drilled it into the stone.

"Not a good day?"

Ester was sat in the shadows to Lux's left. In one hand she had a packet of biscuits and in her other a piece of paper. She joined him.

"What are you doing out here?"

Lux reached for a biscuit. "I needed some quiet."

"Missing your grandpa?"

Lux kicked a stone off the staircase. "And everything else."

Ester gave him a supportive smile.

"I thought Grandpa was just an old man," said Lux numbly. "I didn't realise he'd led the Light Hunters."

"I wish he was here now."

"Me too," said Lux.

A grey lizard scurried across the platform. Lux tapped the paper in Ester's hand. "What's this?"

Ester handed it to him. It was her portrait. She was standing tall, a Gauntlet strapped to her wrist.

"When was this taken?" Lux asked.

"About seventeen years ago."

It took Lux a moment to realise what was wrong about what Ester had said. "How old *are* you?" he asked incredulously.

"Eighteen."

Lux studied the picture. Ester's usual mauve sash looped down from her shoulder. "You looked like *this* when you were one?"

"It's not me."

Lux looked at the portrait again. The figure resembled Ester all right. She had the same shoulder-length, black hair, and arresting blue eyes. And yet, now that she'd drawn his attention to it, Lux could see there were differences. A slightly fuller face, shorter hair, a bigger nose.

"Your mum?" said Lux, catching on.

"Yes."

"She was a Light Hunter?"

"Of course." Ester's eyes sparkled. "She was a Conjuror like Fera, threw a mean *Flame*. Or so I'm told, anyway."

Lux frowned. "So you're told?"

"She died."

Lux made a noise in his throat. "Sorry."

"Don't be." Ester raised her Gauntlet triumphantly. "She gave us this. Not a bad way to go."

"Your mum invented Gauntlets?"

Ester wrinkled her nose. "Not quite. But mum found the

technology in the ruins under Dawnstar. Tesla did the actual inventing."

Lux was still impressed. "How did she die?"

"A Monster got her in the ruins. Her squad brought back what she'd found."

"It's always a Monster," Lux said angrily. He drilled his fist into the stone again. "Deimos is wrong, Ester. Whatever Shade is, it's not the way to stop these things. I won't help him."

"You may not have a choice if he gets to you," said Ester. "Everything my dad told you about Deimos comes from his time with the Light Hunters, but he's grown so much more powerful since he's embraced Shade. No-one's a match for him . . ."

Lux sighed. "Then why are we even trying?"

". . . yet," finished Ester. She looked at Lux. "No-one's a match for him . . . yet. I heard what you did with Bella. *Revive*."

"It was just a cast," dismissed Lux.

Ester grabbed him. "Don't say that. Nobody's been able to throw that cast for decades. If someone was around to cast *Revive* eighteen years ago, my mum would still be alive." Ester let him go. "You can feel sorry for yourself, Lux, but sorry changes nothing. Actions change the world. Listen," she said, "you're a Light Hunter now – we both are. There are creatures out there killing people – creatures my mum gave her life to destroy. The worst of them is Deimos himself. We have to stop him before he kills anyone else."

Lux blinked. Ester's fierce expression reminded him of her days as Miss Hart. Somehow, it made him feel better, like he was back in Daven.

"You always did like telling me off," he joked.

"And you always did like causing trouble."

Ester hooked her arm into Lux's. They sat like this, feeling the cool evening breeze blow across the crater.

Their peace was broken by a rustling sound behind them. Standing by the door was the elevator attendant Lux had spoken to the previous evening.

"Er, Miss Nova," she said nervously, saluting Ester, "your father would like to see you and Lux."

"Tell him we'll be there soon."

The young Hunter wrung her hands. "Miss Nova," she hesitated, "Mr Nova said it was urgent."

Ester opened her mouth to argue but closed it. "Tell him we'll be there in a minute."

The girl saluted smartly and vanished. Ester pushed herself up and brushed a layer of dust from her trousers.

"Well," she said, "looks like it's time to see the boss."

· CHAPTER 39 ·

Lux shuffled into Nova's room alongside Ester and a dozen other Hunters. Nova perched on his desk, greeting his colleagues as they entered. Those already present muttered amongst each other, waiting. Lux and Ester chose seats next to Nova's weapon-rack. Lux had no idea what was happening, but the orderly fashion in which all the other Hunters were entering the room suggested this wasn't the first of such meetings.

"Is that everyone?" Nova checked with the young girl who'd fetched Lux and Ester.

Lux heard a muffled, "Yes."

"Thank you."

A turning lock rang in the silence. Lux looked around at the other Hunters. He was the only one wearing a mauve uniform.

He watched Nova return to his desk, noting dark rings under his eyes.

"Good evening. I am sorry to bring you all here at short notice." He scratched at a day's stubble. "But we have had some concerning news."

The Hunters shifted in their seats.

What news? thought Lux.

"A week ago, we received a note from one of our men in the field. Legau Moreiss." Nova pressed a button on his desk, dimming the room's Light-lanterns. A map appeared on the wall.

"As most of you are aware, Legau patrols the woodland region between Daven and Kofi." The map expanded. Lux recognised a section of land around Daven. "This region is rife with Monster spawn. In the last five years alone Legau has recorded seventy-eight sightings and forty-three kills."

Nova paused, allowing the numbers to sink in.

"His note informed me of a dramatic increase in spawn sightings over the last few months. But more worryingly, it contained a coded reference to a Monster."

Nova gestured and the image changed to depict a four-legged beast, with three thick necks and snarling, open-jawed heads. Each contained two little, dark-red eyes. But it wasn't the eyes that made Lux's breath catch in his throat. What terrified him was a perfectly vertical scar on one of the creature's heads.

A Cerberus.

The Cerberus.

"The more perceptive Hunters amongst you may recognise this

as the beast that decimated Daven ten years ago." Nova glanced at Lux. "Over the last few weeks, Legau has tracked it and spoken to those who have encountered it. It is back, and its lair is in the hills around Kofi."

Lux looked at Ester, unable to comprehend what he was seeing. The Cerberus had been missing for ten years. Most people in Daven had presumed it long dead. But now it was back and threatening Kofi. From where? Why now? And if it was threatening Kofi, it would only be a matter of time before it turned to Daven. Lux thought of his grandpa.

Nova pulled a letter out of his robe pocket. "That was all I had heard. Until this afternoon."

He laid the sheet on his desk and flattened it with his palm. The Cerberus image disappeared, replaced by the letter. Its handwriting was messy, hurried. Lux edged forward.

Artello,

Three bodies. Last two days. Town outskirts. Monster kills. Names: Leroy Nelison, Umbras Weston and Xev Bystand. Send support. Suspect attack imminent.

Legau

"I'm afraid to say I believe Legau is right in presuming the Cerberus is about to attack. As we all know, a Monster making its lair close to a city normally only ends one way. However, there is something even more troubling in this note that Legau could not possibly have seen. Observe the names."

Lux read the note. Leroy Nelison. Umbras Weston. Xev Bystand. He ran their names around his tongue, trying to figure it out. He ventured into his mind, recalling famous Daven and Kofi historical figures. Were any of those called Leroy or Umbras? He didn't think so. There definitely wasn't anyone called Xev. He thought of the two town mayors, and all the rich people who brought their clocks to his grandpa's workshop – still nothing. Frustrated, Lux turned to Ester to see if she'd worked it out. But then he froze. A shiver shot up and down his spine. Under his breath, Lux mouthed the victims' first names, tensing his jaw and trying not to panic.

Leroy.

Umbras.

Xev.

Lux.

· CHAPTER 40 ·

Lux walked closer to the image. The other Hunters watched him as he tested every letter to make sure he hadn't misread any. He was desperate to find a mistake. Surely there had to be something wrong about what he was seeing? He picked the note up off the table.

"What's going on?"

Nova took the note from Lux. "In case any of you are still unsure," he said soberly, addressing the room, "I wish you to look at the first letter of each of the victims' first names." He gave the Hunters time to comply, then pointed to each letter in turn. "L-U-X. Our newest Light Hunter."

An audible gasp travelled the room. All the Hunters looked at Lux, who shrank under their gaze. Over the next few minutes, Nova explained Lux's background – the Cerberus attack, his grandpa, his abilities as a Healer, Deimos's interest in him. His audience listened patiently, glancing at Lux whenever Nova revealed something new.

"And that brings us to now," finished Nova, "and the matter of how we proceed. There is no doubt in my mind that this is a trap. Deimos knew we'd try to get Lux to safety before he even tried to kidnap him from Daven. He set this up to bait Lux out should we succeed. This must not happen." Nova hammered a fist into his desk. "But we cannot abandon Kofi either. Even if the Light Hunters are hated in the region. We must send a squad to assist Legau."

A wave of eager nods swept the room.

"I suggest Squad Juno," said Nova simply. "My daughter has just returned from the region and knows it well. If anyone disagrees, speak now." Nova surveyed his comrades, who remained silent. "Very well. Juno will set off in the morning."

Nova pressed a button on his desk, bathing the room in light again. The Hunters blinked in the sudden glare as Nova resumed his position at the front of the room.

"A lot of you are too young to have known Deimos personally," he said, "but I did. He was a misguided man when he was a Light Hunter, and he's a dangerous man now. Mark my words: Deimos, and his obsession with Shade, is a far greater threat than any Monster in this world. We must be careful. Dismissed."

One by one, all the Hunters shuffled out. Nova stood in front of his desk, his uninjured arm behind his back. Lux and Ester waited for everyone else to leave before they got up.

"You two, wait."

Nova opened the door at the back of his room. A wedge of soft moonlight fell inside, catching his weapons. He rested his good arm on the balcony balustrade and peered into the courtyard. Lux and Ester joined him.

"Thoughts?" said Nova questioningly. His eyes rested on the swaying blossom trees.

Lux had so many thoughts running through his head he could barely stand, let alone speak.

"It's . . . quick," said Ester. "I thought it'd take him longer to come up with something."

"He's a quick man."

"Are you sure one squad will be enough?" she asked dubiously. "If that truly is the same Cerberus from ten years ago . . ."

Nova picked up a pebble and looped it into the fountain below.

"No," he said. "One squad is nowhere near enough. But things are busy now." Nova turned so he was propped up against the rail. "Indeed, while you've been away, there has been an unprecedented rise in Monster attacks, many of which have required our strongest Hunters. Those remaining are teachers, not fighters. As you've just seen. We are short here." He looked at Ester. "It is like Deimos planned it this way."

"Maybe he did."

"Maybe," said Nova thoughtfully. "But the truth is, your mission is to be just a recon mission. Legau is injured. I left that part of the letter out. Some Monster spawn cornered him. They damaged his leg.

"For now, I want you to take your squad and scout the situation.

I have recalled some of my best Hunters, but they are not going to be here for a couple of days."

"So we're just to watch?" said Ester.

"Just find out more. This is clearly a trap. But we need to know if it is merely a trap to get Lux, or whether the Cerberus will indeed attack Kofi."

Nova's reference to Kofi reminded Lux of the times his grandpa had taken him to see the town's zoo, with its giant sabre-toothed cats and flying monkeys. Lux had loved it there. He thought of its upside-down circus, and the world's tallest tree that towered over the concert hall. He thought of the huge, rainbow-flecked waterfalls and lakes. He thought of a trio of children that had chased them down the street, just to hand back Lux's grandpa's misplaced walking cane. The idea that they might undergo a Monster attack – especially one brought about by Deimos – made Lux feel sick.

"We have to get there," he said urgently. "We have to go now."

Nova faced him. "Lux, you can't go."

Lux froze. "What?"

"You can't go," Nova repeated bluntly.

"But . . ."

Ester knelt by Lux. "Deimos is trying to draw you out, Lux," she said softly. "He's going to have people all over."

"But that *thing* killed my family. And . . . and . . . Kofi . . ." In his mind's eye, Lux saw the kids again, chasing his grandpa. He couldn't leave them to fend for themselves. "We have to save them."

"And we will," said Nova.

"But what about healing?" said Lux suddenly. "Legau? Someone needs to heal his leg."

"Legau will be fine. I know that man. He certainly wouldn't trade his safety for yours."

"But . . ."

"Enough!" Nova grew in size before Lux, towering over him. "You are a promising wielder of Light, Lux, but you are *not* ready for this. Deimos is a dangerous man. I promised your grandpa we would keep you safe. I do not intend to break that."

Lux felt tears welling in his eyes. They had to let him go. Even though it was scary, they had to. Why didn't they understand?

"We'll save them," said Ester firmly, wrapping a comforting arm around Lux's shoulder. "And we'll get that *thing*. I promise."

Lux stared at her with red, puffy eyes. Without saying a word, he unhooked himself from her grasp, ducked into Nova's quarters and headed back out to Dawnstar.

· CHAPTER 41 ·

Lux trudged through the corridors, his mind in a daze. He chewed on Nova's decision, clenching his jaw so tight he felt it might snap. It wasn't that Nova and Ester wanted to leave him behind. He understood that. It was their job to look after him. It was their job to look after everybody. Besides, Lux had seen Deimos enough times to know he didn't want to be anywhere near him.

But . . .

But despite the terror that clawed at his insides, there were some things in life more important than fear. Like loyalty. And love. And friendship. And helping people in danger. Lux couldn't leave Kofi to face a Monster attack on its own. If he could save just one person, he had to try.

A sudden urge hit Lux to speak to Maya – someone close to

him, someone who knew what it was like to have a Monster attack your town. He stalked the corridors in search of her. He went first to Tesla's lab, but it was empty. He tried the workshops and cafeteria and library. Still nothing. It was then Lux recalled his and Maya's reunion that morning in Squad Celan's room.

Maya was tweaking a tiny, shell-like gadget at her desk when Lux arrived. "Hey," she said, jumping up, "I've been looking for you."

Aside from Maya, the dorm room was empty. An open window let in a stream of cold air. Lux stomped over and slammed it shut.

"What's up?" asked Maya, concerned.

"This place!" snapped Lux.

"Well, it's not the nicest room in the world, but . . ."

"You know what I mean. Dawnstar."

"What's happened?"

"It's . . ." Lux hesitated. "It's the Cerberus."

"What Cerberus?" As Maya spoke, it dawned on her what Lux meant. Her eyes narrowed.

"The one that attacked Daven. It's back."

"Are you serious?"

"Yes!"

"But it's dead."

"No. It's not."

Maya slumped. ". . . How?"

"I don't know. They've had a letter from some Hunter called Legau. He's seen it near Kofi."

Maya thought. She spread her hands cheerfully. "That's good, isn't it? They'll get it this time."

"No," said Lux impatiently, "you don't understand. It's there because of me. It's killed three people. Their names are a code for my name."

Maya frowned, confused. "Lux?"

"Yes."

Maya walked to the window and back. "This has to be Deimos, right?"

"They think so."

Maya sat next to Lux. "This is all right. We knew he was still going to be after you. Just because you made it to Dawnstar, doesn't mean he'll have given up. At least you're here. You're safe here. Kofi will just have to swallow their pride and let the Hunters help them . . ."

"You don't understand!" said Lux, launching himself up, "I have to go. Those people are in danger because of *me*! And what if it turns on Daven? What about Grandpa? What about school? Your orphanage? Mrs Miggin? Everyone! I can't just sit here. But Nova won't let me go."

Lux thumped the bedside table, knocking off a Gauntlet and sending it tumbling to the floor. His face burned red. He clasped and unclasped his hands, agitated. Maya considered what he'd said. She pushed herself up.

"We have to go," said Lux, reaching out to her suddenly. "We have to sneak out tonight. Warn everyone at Kofi."

"Lux . . ." Maya pulled away.

"All we need is some food, and . . ." Lux picked up the fallen Gauntlet. "And if you can tweak the locator in this to find Kofi . . ."

"Lux..."

He stopped.

"Lux..."

"Please tell me you're not siding with them, Maya."

She rubbed her eyes. "Lux. If anyone can stop that Cerberus, it's the Hunters. If we go on our own, you're not safe anymore. Neither of us would be. Deimos will pick you up before you even get to Kofi. His plan will have worked. And Kofi will probably get attacked anyway." Maya stepped towards Lux, but he backed away. "You know me," she said proudly, "I'm normally first to go on a mission like this. But I think Nova's right. I think we should stay."

Lux looked down at the floor. When he spoke again, his voice was quiet.

"Of all people Maya, I thought you'd understand."

"Lux..."

"No!" A black cloud had descended on him. "All these years I've looked after you. At school, when everyone said you're a dork, I stuck up for you. When no-one wanted to play with you, I did. And now, the one time I need you to do something for me, you let me down. Well I'm going to Kofi," he said angrily, "whether you or the Light Hunters like it or not."

And before Maya could say another word, Lux stormed out. Behind him, the door rattled in its frame, shaking loose a layer of dust.

· CHAPTER 42 ·

Lux returned to Squad Juno's dorm. He'd never felt so miserable and alone. Without Maya, he knew there was no chance of him making it to Kofi that night. In fact, without Maya there was little chance of him making it there at all. How would he know where to go? How would he get there? Maya had a reputation for being a bit ditzy but Lux knew the truth. He'd known it when he'd chosen her to accompany him on his mission to the lighthouse back in Daven. If you wanted to get something done, there was no better partner than Maya Murphy.

Just then, Lux made his choice. He would sneak along to Kofi with the rest of Squad Juno in the morning.

It wasn't ideal. He'd rather have gone immediately. But without Maya, he didn't have many options. Following the others, though risky, was a way to ensure he arrived where he needed to be. A later warning was better than no warning at all.

Lux slept fitfully that night and woke early. To his surprise, Fera and Brace were already up, tiptoeing around him, half-packed satchels lying on their beds. Lux sat up, wiping sleep from his eyes. *Act normal,* he thought.

"Good morning."

Fera and Brace stopped.

"You're awake," said Fera awkwardly.

"I couldn't sleep."

Fera and Brace exchanged a glance.

"I guess Ester's told you the plan," said Lux bluntly.

"Yes."

"It's all right. You don't have to tiptoe around me. I'll just have to come on the next mission."

Fera put down her notebook. "It's pretty awful."

"Hell yeah it is!" said Brace animatedly. "But, honestly, it's probably for the best. Gives you more time to learn the ropes."

Lux said nothing. He slid out of bed and put on his uniform. "How are you getting there, anyway?" he asked as casually as he could, avoiding Fera's eye. He knew Brace wouldn't suspect anything, but Fera he wasn't so sure. "Skyship?"

"We wish." Fera stuffed a spare pair of thermal socks into her satchel.

"What do you mean? How *are* you getting there?"

Brace put a heavy hand on Fera's shoulder. He winked at Lux. "I'm not allowed to say."

"You can," said Fera, shrugging herself free. "He means the teleporter."

"Tele-*what*?" repeated Lux.

"We don't use them often," explained Fera. "Only in emergencies." She grabbed a pencil and started to sketch in her notebook. "It's Light-tech. Ester's mum found it in the ruins beneath the crater when she found the Gauntlet. Every person's made up of Light, you know that, right?" Fera had drawn a small cuboid on the paper. Inside was a person. It looked just like Brace, only with exaggerated ears. "Tesla's worked out a way to dissipate this energy, make it travel and recombine somewhere else."

"So you break apart?" said Lux. He didn't like the sound of that.

"You don't feel it," said Brace, glancing at Fera's drawing and knuckling her playfully in the arm. "It's instantaneous. One second you're here and the next you're somewhere else."

"It's *very* weird," said Fera, shuddering. "I wish we didn't have to do it."

"She really hates it," confirmed Brace.

"It gets the job done," said Fera simply. "It gets us there quick, which is what we need if we want to get to Kofi in time to . . ." She looked up from her drawing at Lux. "Well, you know what I mean."

Fera and Brace resumed packing. Lux stared at Fera's picture, trying to remember what she'd said. He'd been hoping they'd go by skyship. Teleportation sounded like a real challenge.

"Ready?" Fera asked Brace when they'd finished.

"Ready."

Fera faced Lux. "I'm sure Ester wouldn't mind you watching. Do you fancy it?"

"Definitely." Lux feigned a cheeky grin as his insides somersaulted at the opportunity to get near the teleporters. "Any chance to watch my squad-mates go up in a flash of Light."

They made their way out of Squad Juno's dorm and past the busy training rooms, before arriving at the skyship hangar. Fera cast a lingering glance at the ships, then led Lux and Brace down a steep flight of stairs towards Tesla's laboratory.

Tesla was rushing around when they arrived – wheels scraping across the floor, dreadlocks flopping all over his face. Ester was there too, plucking a tiny earpiece out of her ear, squinting at it confusedly and then pushing it in again. In the corner, standing with her arms folded, was Maya. She smiled awkwardly at Lux, who looked away.

"So, you're telling me we can speak to you *on* the mission now?" Ester asked Tesla.

"Yes."

"Not just when we're at Dawnstar?"

"Yes. Maya adjusted the old Shells. They seem to work."

"What's their range?"

Tesla shrugged. "Enough to cover here and Kofi."

"What's going on?" said Brace.

Ester plucked the earpiece out of her ear to show Brace. She stiffened when she saw Lux. Before she could say anything, Fera leapt between them.

"He wants to see the teleporters," she blurted. "I thought it'd be all right."

Lux smiled sweetly at Ester.

"I've seen that smile, Lux Dowd," said Ester, observing him sceptically, "when I caught you stealing cakes from my oven." She tapped a finger rapidly on her thigh, thinking. She pointed to the counter beside her. "If you stay, you stand right there and you don't move an inch."

Inside Lux, fireworks exploded. First step complete.

Tesla and Maya buzzed around them, connecting an increasingly complex web of multicoloured wires to sockets. Fera and Brace sat on the counter next to Lux and listened as Ester explained the changes Maya had made to Tesla's Shell communication system.

"So, we can talk to Tesla?" said Fera interestedly, sliding one of the Shells carefully into her ear.

"That's amazing," added Brace, slotting in his own.

"If it works," said Ester sceptically.

Maya shot them a glance. "It'll work."

Tesla plugged in a final wire and pressed a button. There was a small click and the entire *Blast* chamber wall peeled away, revealing a second, hidden laboratory. Filled with Light of every colour, it was like a rainbow had exploded. Inside were five pods, just like the one Fera had drawn in her notebook. One had its lid up, so Lux could see red velvet lining. Indented in it was an impression of a human body.

A teleporter.

Tesla wheeled into the new laboratory and stopped next to the open cabin. "Who," he said, his eyes twinkling mischievously as he saw the trepidation on Fera and Brace's faces, "wants to go first?"

· CHAPTER 43 ·

Lux waited to see who would volunteer. Ester stepped in front of Fera and Brace, her hands on her hips.

"It's fine," she said reassuringly. "He's fixed it."

Fera and Brace played rock-paper-scissors to see who would go first. Fera chose paper, Brace scissors.

"Ha!" shouted Brace triumphantly, performing a celebratory dance.

Fera barged past him. "I wanted to get it out of the way, anyway."

Tesla offered an arm when she reached the pod. Fera took it and slid inside so she was lying on her back.

"Where are we going to re-form?" she asked.

Tesla looked up from the control panel. "Somewhere in town. Legau's holed up at an inn."

"You can't be more specific?" Fera sat up.

"When you can manipulate a billion particles of Light well enough to transport a squidgy human like you across the region, you can ask me to be more specific." Tesla put a firm hand on her head and pressed her back down.

"Well, excuse me for being cautious," exclaimed Fera indignantly, "but you said the same thing to Karol Dee and you ended up re-forming him underwater!"

Ester sank to her knees by the pod. "Fera, you'll be fine."

"Mmm."

"You're going to get there a little bit before me and Brace. Stay where you are. Wait for us. Anything untoward, you know what to do."

Fera nodded, her expression suddenly focussed. "Yes, boss."

Tesla tapped a final flurry of buttons on Fera's pod, snapped the lid shut and drew across a metal catch. Ester backed up as Lux and Brace edged forwards, peering through the glass. Fera's eyes were squeezed shut.

Tesla clicked a finger at Maya, who was standing next to a button on the wall. Maya pressed it. Immediately, there was a loud *clank* and Fera's pod started shaking. Blue Light sparks flew out, prompting Ester to tap her Gauntlet and generate a *Shield*. Inside the pod, Fera kept her eyes clamped together as a bluish haze surrounded her. Then the pod seemed to implode with a strange *whump-whomp* sound. The Light accompanying all this was so bright Lux had to squeeze shut his eyes too. When he opened them again, Fera was gone. He sidestepped Ester's *Shield* and checked the pod to be sure. But it was true.

"Wow!"

"Lux . . ." The word was drawn out the way his grandpa used to say it when Lux had broken an expensive watch in the workshop. Ester was glaring at him, her arms folded. "We're in a hurry."

Lux dipped his head in apology. *Don't blow it*, he thought, returning swiftly to the counter. Tesla motioned Brace towards the second pod. Brace cupped his ear, listening to his Shell. He smirked.

"I can hear her chuntering. She's not happy."

Brace stepped into the open teleporter. Before lying down, he gripped Tesla's forearm.

"You won't drop me on top of her, will you?" He looked anxiously between Tesla and Ester. "She's already in a bad mood. She'll throw a *Flame* at me. She took off half my hair last time."

Brace twisted to show a shorter patch of hair at the back of his head. Tesla shoved him down and locked the pod. Brace rearranged his backpack and pulled funny faces in the viewing window.

"He'll never grow up," said Ester pityingly.

"They used to say that about you," said Tesla.

This time, as Tesla punched buttons on the control panel, Lux paid close attention, memorising the pattern: red, blue, green, black. He repeated it in his head. *Red, blue, green, black. Red, blue, green, black.* Ester watched him, forcing Lux to look away. Tesla nodded at Maya, still by the switch.

"I'll be happy if you can put this one in the ocean," he muttered.

Maya pressed the button.

Another firework-display lit up the lab, throwing colourful

geometric shapes across Lux's face. It finished with another incandescent flash. Brace was gone.

"There goes two," said Tesla.

Ester shouldered her satchel and turned to him. "Thanks, Tes'," she said, pecking him affectionately on the forehead.

Tesla wriggled out of her grip. "Don't get all soppy on me. Just go and save Kofi."

Ester said goodbye to Lux and Maya and got into the third pod. A few seconds later, she was gone.

Lux was left alone with Tesla and Maya. All three stared silently at Ester's pod.

"You want to go with them, don't you?" said Tesla.

Lux nodded. "I do."

"They don't want you to go."

"I know." Lux glanced quickly at the control panel on the fourth pod. Could he make a run for it? Would they try and stop him?

"You know," said Tesla solemnly, "I've seen a lot of kids come through here with talk of them being the next big thing." He looked up at Lux. "They never are. Oh, they're all talented," he nudged aside a damaged Gauntlet, "but no more than I could make anyone with one of these and a year's training." Tesla wheeled to the fourth pod. "But yesterday, when you threw that *Revive* and brought Bella back, I knew." He looked at the Behemoth statue in the other laboratory. "God knows enough little children have been made orphans. If there's anything you can do to stop it . . ." He delved into his pocket for another Shell earpiece and handed it to Lux. He slapped the pod. "Get in."

Lux put the earpiece in his ear. It crackled lightly. Was this really happening? Was Tesla really going to let him follow them?

"Are you sure?"

"Just get in," said Tesla. "Before I change my mind."

"Thanks," said Lux.

"Don't thank me. Thank her."

Maya fidgeted where she was leaning against the control panel. Lux walked over.

"I thought you said this was a bad idea."

"It is," said Maya stubbornly. "And I think you need to be very careful. But I thought about what you said last night and you were right. You have stuck by me. I guess us orphans have to look out for each other."

"Thank you," said Lux.

"Just go. And make sure nobody gets hurt."

Lux hugged Maya and got into the teleporter. "You won't dump *me* in the ocean, will you?" he asked Tesla.

"Depends. When you get back, will you help me kill that Monster?" Tesla nodded at the statue in his laboratory.

Lux grinned. For the first time since arriving at Dawnstar, he felt like a real Light Hunter.

"Definitely."

"Then I'd say we're good."

With that, Tesla slammed Lux's teleporter shut. Maya pressed the button and blasted Lux into a million particles of Light.

· CHAPTER 44 ·

For a brief moment, Lux ceased to be. An intense darkness surrounded him. All was silent. Then an awareness came – a sensation – and Lux could feel again. The space around him morphed from endless night to stunning day – sparks and stars and novas. Lux shot through this, all the points becoming streaks. Only one spot remained stationary – a white, inflating dot ahead of him. Lux fixed himself on this, until finally the brightness became so overwhelming he had to turn from it in his mind.

When Lux came to, he was levitating a metre off dusty ground. He flapped his arms desperately, trying to get some purchase on the floor. But he fell, impacting the earth with his left flank and knocking the wind out of him.

Well it wasn't underwater at least, he thought.

To Lux's left, a stream rippled by, and in the distance he could hear children laughing. A nearby bridge shaded him from the morning sun. Beyond, Kofi's twin waterfalls fell from the sky, tossing plumes of white spray up the towering cliffs.

Lux took in the town's familiar sights – the waterfalls and lakes, the bustling market and all the friendly people. Kofi had always been one of his favourite places. He could have stayed there all day, allowing the morning sun to gently warm him. But a sudden awareness came to him that Ester, Fera and Brace had teleported a few minutes earlier. He looked around but they were nowhere to be seen.

To Lux's right, the river meandered out of town, climbing a lush valley. To his left, the stream straightened to a canal, arrowing into the heart of Kofi. Suddenly, Lux recognised where he was. He peered downstream and located the enormous gold dome that crowned the town's zoo. Sitting in its shadow, much to Lux's astonishment, was Brace.

Before Lux could catch his squad-mate's attention, the Shell in his ear hissed. ". . . ow's he going to hear me if I don't speak?"

It was Maya.

"You're not *meant* to be speaking at all," said Tesla gruffly, his voice crackling in static.

"Hello?" said Lux.

"Ah, there you are." Tesla sounded relieved. "We were starting to wonder if you'd made it."

"I'm here."

"This is a private channel," said Maya. "The others can't hear you."

"Depending on where you've landed," said Tesla, "you're going to want to head towards town. Legau's holed up there."

"I can see them," said Lux.

"You can?"

"Well, Brace anyway."

There was silence on the other end of the Shell, then Tesla's voice. "Well, what are you doing talking to us then? Go and catch up with them!"

The hissing in Lux's ear vanished. Jogging downstream, Lux dodged scattered rocks as he scanned the plaza around the zoo. Sure enough, he picked out Fera too, playing with a floppy-eared dog, and Ester, chatting to a local.

Boy are they in for a surprise, he thought, with just a hint of trepidation.

Lux descended a staircase that opened into the sloped streets. Fera saw him first and almost did a double-take. She smiled happily. Returning from the Kofi local, Ester saw Fera's smile and looked in Lux's direction. Her face grew instantly stormy. She clicked a finger for Fera and Brace to follow.

Lux limped towards them, the pain from his fall still stabbing his hip. They met outside an alley by the zoo. Without a word, Ester half-lifted, half-dragged Lux inside and shoved him up against the wall. She'd never looked madder.

"What are you *doing* here?"

Lux squirmed, uncomfortable.

"It was Tesla, wasn't it?"

"He was only trying to help."

"That damn man," said Ester furiously. "He never does what he's told."

The Shell in Lux's ear hissed. "I can hear you, you know?" came Tesla's reply.

Ester threw a finger to her ear. "Oh, you're there, are you? Would you mind telling me what you were thinking?"

"Ester, I knew you'd be mad . . ."

"Mad doesn't even begin to cover it, Tes'. Lux was supposed to stay at Dawnstar for a reason."

Tesla sighed heavily. "Ester, can you remember when your mother's squad got back after their raid on the ruins and they told us she'd died? Can you remember what you wanted to do?"

"That's different," said Ester sharply.

"Hmm . . ."

Ester touched the Shell in her ear, switching it off.

Lux shrank against the wall. "I'm sorry," he said quietly. "I had to come." He wasn't sorry at all, but it seemed like the right thing to say.

Ester rounded on him. "Lux, this whole thing's a trap. The Cerberus, Kofi, all of it. The point was to get you here. And you've come!" She lowered her voice. "Deimos will have people all over town looking for you. I'll be surprised if one of them hasn't seen you already."

Fera and Brace exchanged a puzzled glance. "Deimos?" Fera enquired.

"I'm sorry," Lux said. "But I had to come."

"My father expressly told you not to!"

"I know!" Lux slumped against the wall. Did she think he didn't know that? "But . . . I thought you'd understand."

"Lux, you shouldn't have . . ."

"Wait!" Lux cut Ester off. "Two nights ago, I was a normal kid. Then things flipped upside-down. I've got Deimos chasing me, you take me to Dawnstar and everyone tells me I'm some special, amazing Healer. Kofi gets attacked, because of *me*! And you all expect me to sit there twiddling my thumbs. No!" Lux jumped up. "My grandpa didn't get me out of Daven so I could sit in Dawnstar." He looked at his hands. "If I'm such a good Healer . . . well, we've got a great squad." He glanced at Fera and Brace, who were both smiling proudly. "And we should go and take this Cerberus out. Then Deimos!"

Lux had gone red and he was almost panting. Ester stared at him, measuring the emotion behind his words. She burst out laughing.

"What's so funny?" snapped Lux.

"Nothing. It's just you remind me of him. When he used to grump at me for forgetting to add wine to the stew."

Lux smiled.

"Listen," said Ester wearily, "if you really want to stay, I won't stop you. God knows what trouble it'll get me in, but I won't."

"Someone's got to push back," said Lux.

"Said like a true Dowd. All right . . ." Ester faced Fera and Brace. ". . . looks like we've got a full squad again, guys."

"Wicked!" said Brace. "Just one problem. So far, I've heard about Deimos, incredibly talented Healers and someone's grandpa, but

I'm going to be honest, I have absolutely no idea what's going on."

To his left, Fera nodded in agreement.

"So," Brace went on, "would one of you please tell us what we've let ourselves in for?"

· CHAPTER 45 ·

Lux kept guard at the alley entrance as Ester told Fera and Brace the full story.

"I didn't realise we were with Light Hunter royalty," Brace said to Lux once Ester had finished. "I'd have bowed if I'd known." He bowed now, making Lux laugh. Light Hunter royalty? Lux prayed that wouldn't stick.

Fera came next. "A special Healer, eh?" She tilted her head, weighing its worth. "Just don't go healing any Monsters I blast apart." She winked.

"Right," Ester cut in impatiently, pushing past them. "We'd better get to Legau before he thinks we've abandoned him."

On constant lookout for Deimos or his people, Ester guided them cautiously to the centre of town. Kofi was much as Lux remembered it. The main road was lined with noisy pedlars, selling their wares. The houses and shops resembled those in Daven – wooden and rickety, with tall spires that punctured the sky. Back at the roadside, green permeated everything. Weeds burst through pavement cracks and leaves overhung the roads.

However, Kofi's true marvel was its waterfalls. So arresting were they that even Ester paused to stare whenever they had a decent view. Two enormous, white, tumbling sheets bracketed the town like book-ends. In the sunlight, they were the most beautiful things Lux had ever seen.

At the centre of town, they came upon a compact market square, packed with rundown little stalls. Ester checked the area, trying to spot anyone suspicious. Lux picked out one sullen-looking, pipe-smoking man with a facial scar perched on a wooden fence. He tugged Ester's sleeve.

"If that was all we had to worry about," scoffed Ester, "I could go home and leave you three to it." She scanned the crowd once more and snapped her fingers for them to huddle. "Don't look now," she whispered, "but Legau's in that inn over there. The Howling Hydra."

Lux glanced at the inn. Ester glared at him. "I said *don't* look." She shook her head. "I'll lead us in. You three, keep behind me. Anyone speaks to you, point them to me. Got it?"

Lux, Fera and Brace nodded.

"All right, let's go."

Ester led them through the market to the Howling Hydra – a tattered-looking, two-storey building at the north end of the square. Inside, Lux was immediately overwhelmed by pipe smoke, so thick it reminded him of Tesla's laboratory after the *Blast* explosion. He wafted a hand and joined Ester at the counter. An old barmaid there looked up wearily from her cross-stitch, her eyes drawn to Ester's Gauntlet.

"And I suppose *you're* a travelling gardener too, like the other one?" she said sarcastically.

"That's right," smiled Ester. "These are my workers."

Lux, Fera and Brace waved.

"Hmm." The barmaid put her cross-stitch on a footstool and groaned as she struggled to her feet. "As long as you prune that big plant that's been causing trouble outside town, your type are all right with me."

Ester thanked her. The lady came out from behind the counter and hobbled towards a side door. She eased it open and jerked a thumb at the stairway beyond.

"Up there, second room on your left." She grabbed Ester's wrist, her face serious. "He's been in there three days. He's hurt pretty bad, but he won't accept any help."

Fera made it to the top of the staircase first. Ester reached out and tugged her back. On the landing, she checked nobody was watching, then whispered, "You've never met Legau. He's . . ." She grasped for the right word, ". . . well, he's a little more *traditional* than most Hunters. If he comes across as *odd*, don't take it personally."

Odd? wondered Lux.

Ester slipped down the corridor and stopped outside the

second room on the left. She knocked. Lux heard a soft rustling sound, then a clipped, gruff voice. "If another of you kids asks me to play cards . . ."

"Legau, it's me," whispered Ester urgently. "We've come to rescue you."

· CHAPTER 46 ·

The door swung open into a large room, furnished with twin antique beds and wardrobes. Two arched windows gave a view of the square below. One was open, so that Lux could hear the bustling market sellers below. Pale, yellow sunlight highlighted a mountain of junk on the floor – jackets, armour, a dagger, books, two empty plates and a pile of cigar ash. A trail of this led to the bed. Lying on the mattress, his left leg elevated on a small wooden chest, was Legau Moreiss.

"You've come to rescue me?" he said incredulously. "And what makes you think I *need* rescuin'? In fact, I was just about to give that three-headed puppy the lickin' of its lifetime!"

"You wrote to us!" said Ester, pecking him on the forehead.

"I meant for your pop to send some real Hunters. Not Little

Bo-Peep and her three lambs." Legau cast a withering glance over Lux, Fera and Brace.

Ester examined his injured leg, which Lux thought looked as bad as Maya's after her encounter with the Monster spawn. "Are you all right?"

"Does it look like it?"

Legau was a tall man with long, unkempt, grey-blonde hair and a bushy moustache. His skin was tanned and lined like leather, crossed with old burns and scars. He wore a faded, red-and-black checked shirt and big, heavy boots. His nose was long and hooked, crooked where it had been broken. He looked just like pictures of old Light Hunters Lux had seen in his sister's books.

Ester squinted in the sunlight. She went to the arched windows and drew the curtains.

"Who are they anyway?" demanded Legau bluntly, nodding at Lux, Fera and Brace. "Because I ain't playin' cards . . ."

"You know darn well who they are," said Ester, scooping objects off the floor and dumping them in the wardrobe.

"Oh, I forgot. Your old man's great drive for the future." He chewed his moustache. "Bunch of tosh. Light Hunters should be men like me. Fit." He puffed out his chest. "In their prime."

Brace leapt up, desperate to point out the irony of Legau's words, but Fera tugged him back.

"No wonder everyone around here hates us," Legau went on bitterly, reaching to his bedside table for a cigar and throwing a small *Flame* cast to light it. "We're sendin' out children!"

"Nice to know a bit of time in beautiful Kofi hasn't changed you one bit," said Ester sarcastically. She plucked the cigar from between Legau's lips and snuffed it out on the bedside table.

"Well," said Legau, shifting on his mattress, "it's Monsters we're talkin' about, Ester – big, scary blighters. I don't know about you, but every kiddie I've ever known has shaken in their boots at the thought of them." Legau twizzled his moustache. Lux got the sense he was half-playing with Ester, half telling the truth.

"Shut it, old man," said Ester affectionately. She stripped back the fabric of his trousers and revealed his wound – a ragged slash from knee to ankle. Fera and Brace flinched.

Ester motioned Lux over.

"Oh no, no, no," said Legau nervously, waving his hands in protest, "he'll probably singe me with a *Bolt* or somethin'."

Ester silenced him with a glare. Lux stepped into position and placed his hands in front of his chest, readying a *Heal* cast. As threads of Light coalesced between his fingers, Ester turned Legau's head away.

"Tell me what happened."

Legau wrinkled his nose. "Ain't much to tell, if I'm honest." He winced as the first Light particles broke on his skin. "I got ambushed by Monster spawn while out lookin' for that big feller, and . . ." He tapped his leg.

"One Monster spawn?" said Brace, unimpressed. He conjured his Light-bow and mimed firing an arrow. "I could have shot it a mile off."

"There were a dozen," Legau replied sharply. "Not often you see 'em clustered like that. Think an attack on the town's comin'."

Legau's words shot a lump into Lux's throat. He had to concentrate to keep control of his cast.

"So does my father," said Ester.

"Where's the rest of you then?"

"We're it, for now."

Legau burst out laughing. "You're kiddin'?"

"It's a recon mission," explained Ester defensively. "We're here to see where the Monster is, find its lair and report back."

"I did make it clear in my letter, didn't I? This is the same Cerberus that smashed up Daven. I don't know if you remember but sendin' one squad didn't work out so well then."

"Listen," said Ester wearily, "we didn't come here for a lecture. We came because you're our best chance of finding the Cerberus. Are you going to help or not?"

Lux had finished his *Heal* and he stepped away from the bed. The others leaned in to look at Legau's leg. The wound had completely healed.

"I don't think you'll be able to walk for a bit," Lux advised hesitantly. "But it should be fixed."

Legau sat up. He ran his hand up his shin, tapping every few centimetres to test the pain. He grunted, impressed.

"I don't know where the damn thing is," he barked grouchily, rearranging his hat as he lay down again. "I tracked it for weeks, but I never really got close."

"Then how're we meant to find it?" asked Brace.

"If you'd let me finish, you'll find out. There is someone in town who's seen it. A young woman. A cartographer."

"A car-what?" said Lux. He'd heard of the word but had no idea what it meant.

"A map-maker," explained Fera.

"She was mappin' the mountains past the waterfalls. Saw it out there."

"How sure are we this is real?" said Ester sceptically.

Legau shrugged. "Do you have any other options?"

"I suppose not. Where is she?"

"Lives in a hut near the Monster watchtower on top of the cliff. I'll warn you though, she's not Kofi's most helpful person. She can be quite a pain in the backside, if I'm honest."

Ester grinned. "Reminds me of someone else round here."

· CHAPTER 47 ·

Having got the information she needed, Ester nudged Lux, Brace and Fera towards the door. But Legau stopped them. He insisted they stay while he ordered some food.

"I've been a Light Hunter for thirty-seven years," he said coolly. "You don't head out on a mission without a full stomach."

They ate with him – piles of cheese and ham sandwiches, crisps and baked apple-pie and ice cream. It all tasted amazing – salty and sweet and delicious. And it dawned on Lux, as he sat chomping away with Fera and Brace, that with all that had happened, he was forgetting what it felt like to have fun.

Legau looked down at the kids from the bed. "Lords alive," he said to Ester, "they eat a lot, don't they?" He glanced mournfully at the rapidly diminishing pile of sandwiches. "Leave some for me, you little rugrats."

When they'd finished, Ester thanked Legau. Then Fera and Brace shouldered their satchels and Ester led them out, checking both ways before proceeding. As Lux left, Legau barked his name.

"Thanks for my leg, kid."

Ester, Fera and Brace had already returned to the ale-room when Lux reached the hall. He headed towards the staircase but stopped when he heard a voice.

"Hey!"

A trio of boys appeared, dressed in frayed clothes and mud-splattered shoes. One was carrying a battered pack of playing cards. "Is he in?" he asked eagerly, nodding at Legau's door.

"You know what?" said Lux mischievously, "he was just saying how much he fancied a game."

The last thing Lux heard, as he entered the ale-room, was a loud groan from Legau as the boys shut his door behind them.

The bar had mostly cleared in the time they'd been with Legau. The blanket of smoke had lifted, leaving the place looking sad, dark and dingy. The others stood at the counter – Brace and Fera playing with a wooden games machine as Ester spoke with the innkeeper. Her eyes were grim, concerned. Something was wrong.

"Where was it found?" she asked anxiously.

"I don't know," said the old lady. "You'd have to ask a newsboy. One of our locals just told me."

"You're sure his name was Darnem?"

"Darnem Bulwell," the innkeep confirmed. "Pleasant lad. Delivered all our ale until we got a cart of our own."

Ester turned away, a pensive look on her face.

"What is it?" Fera asked.

"Another body. Darnem Bulwell."

"Darnem?" exclaimed Brace. "That's L-U-X D-."

"That leaves three," said Lux.

"Which means we don't have long." Ester put a copper shailing on the counter. "Come on, we'd better get up to that cartographer."

Outside the Howling Hydra, the square was set in shadow. The sun had disappeared behind cloud now, and Lux had to pull his jacket tight to stop himself shivering. It reminded him of the day he'd visited Kofi with his grandpa a few years before. Beyond the market square's towering buildings, the twin waterfalls still tumbled – huge, grey anvils lingering malevolently over town.

Fera spotted them first – three gruff men with tattoos on their necks. She tugged Ester's sleeve as subtly as she could, pointing them out. They were dressed to blend in with all the townspeople – faded shirts, scruffy trousers. But there was no mistaking it, the men were with Deimos.

The strangers noticed Ester and the kids and eased themselves off a waist-high wall, skulking menacingly towards them. Fera and Brace moved silently into position beside Ester. Brace was just conjuring his Light-bow when Ester stopped him.

"Fera and I have fought Shade before," she said, rolling up her sleeve and tapping at her Gauntlet. "You two get to the cartographer," she ordered Lux and Brace, "we'll take care of these."

"But won't you need a Heal . . ." started Lux, but Brace grabbed him and pulled him away. Together, they swerved through the market-stalls, knocking over stands of fruits and vegetables. Lux kept glancing behind him, trying to focus on the battle, but it was impossible to see what was happening amongst the firework display of blue and red Light. They reached the exit. Brace selected an empty street and grabbed Lux again.

Lux tugged back. What was Brace playing at? "We've got to help them."

"We *need* to follow orders," said Brace sharply.

Lux looked apprehensively at the whizzing colours, shaking his head. Surely they'd all be better sticking together? But in the end he followed Brace, trying hard to do as he was told. He'd already annoyed Ester by sneaking along to Kofi; he didn't want to make things worse.

When they entered the adjoining street, Brace finally slowed his pace, gesturing for Lux to do the same. He stopped by a short, bearded street-pedlar, waiting for him to serve a customer, then swiped a pair of hats from his stand. He flicked one deftly onto his head and tossed the other – a grey, woollen beanie – to Lux. Lux stared, amazed. How had he ended up with the criminal of Squad Juno?

"What?" said Brace defensively. "I told you they got me from the streets."

They continued along, glancing back in case any of Deimos's people were following, then traversed a walkway over the river. Lux paused. Brace stopped too when he could no longer hear

Lux's footsteps. He turned, his fists bunched, ready to strike. But he relaxed when he saw they were safe.

"Come on!" he called impatiently.

Lux pulled away. He needed to think.

"Lux . . ." warned Brace.

"Wait!" Lux lowered his voice. "We're going up there, right?" He indicated the waterfalls, further upstream.

"That's the plan."

Lux thought back to his trips to Kofi with his grandpa. They'd visited the waterfalls back then too. He was sure there was another route, something a little more hidden. Lux racked his brain.

"I've got it," he said, "I know a short-cut."

Lux guided Brace down the riverbank, weaving between boulders. Soon, they felt a fine mist from the waterfalls on their skin. When they reached the first lake's shore, Lux pulled up. It had been around here, hadn't it? He crossed to a nearby willow tree and parted its branches. A rocky path ran around the lake to the cliff-face, left of the first waterfall. From there, it branched out – one spoke leading to the second lake and the other to a staircase in the cliff-wall. *Got it!* he thought.

Brace traced the narrow steps all the way up the cliff with an undisguised look of despair.

"Next time," he groaned, "remind me to stay and fight."

· CHAPTER 48 ·

After their flight from the inn, hauling their bodies up the foothigh increments that formed the cliff staircase was a devastating challenge. Lux's thighs burned, and he felt a dull ache in his hip where he'd banged it teleporting. *Maybe rematerialising underwater really would have been better,* he thought. Brace moved with equal difficulty – quickly scaling a dozen steps and then stopping to catch his breath.

"Did I ever tell you I hate heights?" he said miserably, leaning against the cliff and sucking in air.

"Didn't you say you want to be a pilot?" asked Lux.

"That's different."

"Well, you're going to love the next few minutes."

To their right, the waterfall raged, a torrent of white spray that drenched Lux and Brace, pinning their clothes to their skin. Below, murky blue water reflected a wall of grey clouds. Beyond, the river slid through green banks before merging with the red and brown town.

"It's not that I feel like I'm going to fall off or anything," said Brace musingly as he re-spiked his hair. "It's just that I don't like seeing things so . . . well, small. Makes me a bit dizzy.

"This is what it must be like to be a Monster," he added, peeking over the edge.

"Maybe," said Lux absently. Although, truthfully, he'd never really thought about what it might be like to be a Monster.

When they set off again, Lux looked back along the river every few steps to see if he could spy Fera or Ester. No sign. He did see a group of three men stumbling towards the falls though. Were they Deimos's people? Had they managed to defeat the girls back at the market? He quickly lost them amongst the trees.

Soon, a spire appeared on the horizon. Then more. Lux realised one was Daven's clock-tower – its illuminated clockface a blank, silver disc in the gloom. He could make out the lighthouse too – a matchstick against the sea's endless blue. Even this close, Lux felt a long way from home.

He noticed Brace staring. "Is that it?" he asked solemnly. "Home-town of the famous Lux Dowd?"

Lux nodded.

"I went to Daven once. My uncle was a Light Hunter. Used to take us around until he went missing."

"Missing?"

"Long story," explained Brace. "Now's probably not the time. It left me and my brother on the streets though. We lived in Kofi and spent a few months in Daven. Nice place. We'll have to go back someday."

Lux imagined the Cerberus rampaging through Daven's streets. He thought of his grandpa. *I hope not.*

"Can I ask you something?" said Lux. "How did you become a Light Hunter? I mean, how did you even learn?"

"My uncle taught me before he disappeared." Brace climbed a steep step. "Then I stopped for a bit. It's only when I wanted to know what had happened to him that I started doing it again. So I joined the Light Hunters."

"You just joined? Like that?"

"Well, they were scouting around and I let it be known I was interested. I mean," he spread his arms theatrically, "you're not going to turn *me* down, are you?"

"Absolutely not," said Lux, arching an eyebrow. "Did you find out what happened? To your uncle?"

"Not yet. But I'm looking. Like I say, I'll tell you about it all when we've got more time."

Lux made it to the top of the cliff first, levering himself over and collapsing in a heap. Together, he and Brace sucked in cool air, their chests pumping. Lux's breathing finally slowed and he dragged himself up.

"Come on," he said impatiently. "They might have gone a different way. We need to get there in case they're waiting."

"Damn," grumbled Brace, climbing wearily to his feet. "And I thought Ester was a slave-driver."

Grassland peeled away from the cliff, slowly turning to dense forest. Lux and Brace threaded their way through until they stumbled upon a rough-cut path.

"Looks like we're getting somewhere," said Lux.

"Worth a go," agreed Brace.

They followed the path past old, crumbling stone houses and through a series of muddy rises and dips until they spied a clearing in the trees. Soaring out of it was a grand Monster watchtower like Daven's – lined with windows and topped by a viewing globe and a huge onyx spire. A walkway wound around the outside, leading to the top. Lux watched it for signs of people.

"Can you see the cartographer's hut?" he whispered to Brace.

Brace poked his head into the clearing. "It's over there," he said, nodding to Lux's left.

A tiny, dilapidated wooden shack stood at the end of a dirt track. It had a sloped, threadbare roof, painted green to blend in with its surroundings.

"You don't think she lives in there, do you?" said Lux.

"Why not?" said Brace a touch defensively. "I lived in something just like that when I was little."

Lux checked to see whether Brace was joking. "Really?"

"Not everyone's born with a silver spoon, Lux."

"I didn't mean . . ." said Lux feebly, but Brace's face collapsed to a grin.

"I'm only yanking your chain," he said. "I'm not bothered. I did live somewhere like that, though." He spun, gesturing proudly to himself. "I turned out all right, didn't I?"

Lux laughed.

Half an hour passed as they waited for Fera and Ester. Lux felt a buzz of nervousness. He tried sitting down, standing, pacing – nothing helped. They were taking too long. Surely they should have made it by now? After a while, he tapped his Shell and put in a call to Ester, just to be sure. He listened for the tell-tale hiss to say she'd picked up but heard nothing.

Come on, he thought, *somebody answer.*

Adjusting the frequency, he tried Tesla and Maya at Dawnstar. Still nothing. "The Shell seems to be down."

"They've never worked properly," said Brace.

Lux stared into the clearing. "What if they need help? I think we should go back."

Brace was sitting on an upturned log, idly cleaning his boots with a conjured Light-dagger. He flicked the blade at Lux and a spark of blue Light drifted slowly between them. "They won."

Just then, they heard the sound of snapping twigs and rustling leaves. Lux's heart lurched in his chest as Brace leapt up, conjuring his Light-bow and aiming an arrow. Was it Ester and Fera? Or the men he'd seen by the river? Lux thought he heard a deep voice and he nudged Brace for them to retreat into the clearing. Brace shrugged him off.

"Never run," he whispered fiercely.

"But don't get trapped either," said a voice directly to their left.

Lux and Brace froze. Standing there, a razor-sharp Light-blade extended from her Gauntlet, was Ester. Beside her, a *Bolt* cast resting nestled in her chest and an amused grin on her face, was Fera.

· CHAPTER 49 ·

Brace dismissed his Light-bow and blew air through his lips, relieved. "Holy moly," he said, "you guys scared me."

"It's all right saying not to run," chided Ester, retracting her Light-blade as Fera dismissed her *Bolt*, "but you've got to be prepared for anything." She paced to the clearing and spotted the Monster watchtower. "Have you been watching?"

"Yes," said Brace.

"Anything?"

"We've not seen anyone."

"What about the shack?"

Lux pointed it out.

"If we're going to speak to this cartographer," said Ester,

"there's a good chance Deimos's people will know about her too. Keep your wits about you."

"What about those men?" said Lux. "Did you beat them?"

"They're . . ." Ester and Fera both smirked. "Let's just say we cast a bit of Light on their Shade."

Ester slipped past them all into the clearing. Up close, the shack was even more of a wreck than it had appeared from the woods, with loose panels, chipped paint and boarded-up windows. A rusted bicycle was propped against one wall and Lux could see patches of mould. How could anyone live like that?

Ester stopped when she reached the porch. "Remember," she whispered urgently, "Legau said she'd be hard work. Be polite." She looked pointedly at Brace. "And if you can't do that, be quiet."

Ester climbed the stairs, removing her hand from the bannister when she saw woodworms spilling out. She knocked on the door. Lux cupped his ear, listening for any movement. He heard a loud bump, then a shuttered window snapped open and abruptly closed.

"Go away, I don't want visitors." The voice was sharp. It belonged to a young woman.

"My name's Ester," she said amiably through the door. "I'm a Light Hunter. This is my squad." She listened for a response. No answer. "Legau sent us." Ester listened again. She shrugged. "Hello?"

"I told you to go away," snapped the girl. "I told Legau I didn't want to talk to anyone."

Ester leaned on the door-frame. "We're here to talk about the Cerberus. We want to stop it."

"You're not supposed to be out here. None of you lot are. And I'm not supposed to be talking to you."

Ester breathed slowly and deliberately, mastering her frustration. "Is it true what Legau said? Did you see a Cerberus?"

Lux heard the door unlatch. It swung slowly inwards. Had they got through? Standing there was a pretty, blonde-haired girl of about Ester's age. She wore thick-lensed spectacles and her khaki clothes were smart. Around her waist hung a utility belt, stuffed with pencils, pens, rulers and rubbers. She stepped closer, so that her face was a few inches from Ester's.

"I said," she snarled, forcing her words through gritted teeth, "I don't want visitors. Now, get off my property, go back to whatever Light hole you crawled from and leave me alone."

The girl held Ester's gaze, then ducked back inside and slammed her door. Ester clumped down the stairs.

Lux watched all this from a distance. His mind was focussed on the girl. He'd met her somewhere before. He perched on the rusted bicycle, trying to remember.

"Are you all right?" asked Fera.

"Shh. I'm thinking."

The only place Lux could possibly have met her was in his grandpa's workshop. He ran through all their customers in his mind, picturing them. Was she one of the young ladies who brought in broken watches from the old peoples' home? Or was she the council girl always trying to get his grandpa to modernise the sign outside his shop? No . . .

Lux had her.

She'd visited the workshop half a year before with a broken compass. The instrument had stuck in Lux's mind because it was made of solid gold and inscribed with an intricately-carved lion. She'd told him she was from Kofi, too, now that he thought about it. Was it Manda? Something like that. Candy? Or Carly? Cind . . .

Cinda!

The exchange flooded back to Lux as if it had happened yesterday. Would she remember it though? Lux opened his eyes and found Ester, Fera and Brace huddled nearby, staring at him. He ignored them and knocked on the door. The girl didn't answer so he rapped again, harder.

"Hello?"

"I told you . . ." snapped the girl, opening the door and brandishing a telescope, "to leave me alo . . ."

She paused, peering curiously down at Lux. She lowered the scope.

"Cinda Fosvid," he said confidently. Now that he could see her up close, he knew it was definitely her. "You came to my grandpa's clock repair shop in Daven a few months ago with your compass. We fixed it."

Cinda cocked her head. "Are you Ben Dowd's boy?"

Lux nodded.

Cinda seemed to think. She opened her mouth to ask a question. "Are you..?" She paused, looking beyond the Monster watchtower into the valley, a puzzled expression warping her face. "You can have twenty minutes," she said grudgingly, stepping aside to let them enter.

· CHAPTER 50 ·

Lux had seen some odd places in his short life, but no place was stranger than the inside of Cinda's shack.

There were maps *everywhere.*

They carpeted the floor and walls. They adorned tables. They hung on chairs. They were stuffed in bins. They were rolled up and used as flower vases. They poked out of books and smouldered as embers in a fire. There were globes too, ranging in size from Lux's fist to his head. Scattered amongst all of these were tools – rubbers, pencils, tape-reels, measures, notepads, scissors, clips and compasses and some contraptions Lux had never seen.

Lux picked his way through the mess, selecting a spot on a small sofa by the fire. Ester, Fera and Brace joined him as Cinda shut the door. The room smelled damp and was lit by a single oil lantern over Cinda's desk. Without speaking, she pulled four cracked mugs from a cupboard and made teas from a black kettle by the fire.

"What exactly is it you want to know?"

Lux, Ester, Fera and Brace exchanged uncertain glances, deciding who would speak first. Ester leaned forward. "Legau told us you saw the Cerberus," she said, accepting a sweet-smelling drink from Cinda. She offered the same to Lux, Fera and Brace. "We want to know what you saw, anything at all you think might help."

Cinda fiddled with a pair of compasses. "There's not a whole lot to tell," she said blankly. "You know there was an earthquake here last year, right?"

"We saw some damaged buildings near the cliff," said Brace.

"A lot of the land above town was jumbled up. Rock-slides. Floods. It really changed things."

Now that Lux thought about it, he could remember the buildings, as well as fallen trees and fresh boulders. An earthquake made sense. Although thinking back to the previous year, he'd felt nothing in Daven.

Cinda put down the compasses and picked up a pencil. She started doodling on a notepad.

"A lot of people have been getting lost, so a few weeks ago I thought I'd hike up into the valley and see if I could sketch a new map. There's not a ton of money in cartography, so any chance to earn a few shailings . . . Anyway, I'd mapped just as far as the Iron Foot . . ."

"The *what*?" said Fera.

"It's a spur of rock a mile up in the valley. I'd got as far as that, when something hit my skyship . . ."

"You have a skyship?" said Brace excitedly.

"I *had* a very small one. My dad's." Cinda glared at Ester. "Are they going to keep interrupting me, or are you going to let me tell you what happened?"

"They'll be quiet."

"When I woke up, I was in a clearing like this one, only with a waterfall and a shallow pool. The next thing I know, I hear this blood-curdling roar. A huge creature bursts out of the trees and charges at me.

"I was too groggy to move, so it hit me head on. Fortunately, it smashed me into a cave behind the waterfall."

"Fortunately," echoed Lux. It didn't sound so fortunate. Especially to Lux, who had a sudden flashback to his and Maya's Monster attack.

"What happened next?" asked Ester.

"It stomped around outside, trying to find me. I watched it through the waterfall – big, horrible thing."

"How did you get away?"

"After a while, it gave up stalking me and slept in the pool. Then, at some point in the night, it disappeared. That's when I got out."

"How did you find your way back?" asked Fera.

Cinda put down her pencil. "I'm a cartographer."

Ester digested everything Cinda had said. Lux looked up at the map-maker, who smiled awkwardly back at him.

"Can you describe more about the Monster?" asked Ester. "How big? Claws? Stuff like that."

"I can do you one better." Cinda tore off the top sheet of her notepad and turned up the lantern flame, casting a warm, orange glow across the cabin. Sketched on the sheet was a perfect image of her shack, next to an equally perfect image of a Cerberus, its three heads twisting and straining.

"Is that to scale?" asked Lux incredulously. If it was, then the Cerberus was bigger even than he'd ever imagined, even in his nightmares.

"She wouldn't have bothered drawing the shack if it wasn't," said Fera, nudging Brace aside to get a better look.

Brace whistled. "That thing is *big.*"

Ester silenced them all with a glare. Cinda tapped a pencil on the Cerberus. "I have him to thank for this." She untucked her shirt, revealing a long scar on her hip. Healed, Lux noticed, but substantial.

Ester reached for the image. "Do you mind?"

"Go ahead."

Ester took the note as Cinda lowered her shirt, gathered up their four empty mugs and washed them in the sink.

"I have a map," she blurted suddenly. "To its lair."

Ester pocketed the drawing and looked at the cartographer, interested.

"I drew it when I got back." Cinda dried her hands on a rag and unhooked a brown leather satchel from her chair. "But then you've got to go. And don't tell anyone I spoke to you."

Cinda glared at Ester until she agreed.

Retrieving a piece of paper from her bag, she flattened it on her desk. It was hard to see in the dim light, but Lux could make out Kofi's waterfalls, woods and the valley behind the Monster watchtower. A red, dotted line ended at a large patch of blue and green, marked with a cross.

The Monster's lair.

Ester positioned her Gauntlet over the page. There was a flash of Light and a copy of the map appeared above the gadget. Ester checked to make sure her Gauntlet's image matched Cinda's.

"That was Light, wasn't it?" said Cinda. "My dad ran the Light cable-cars behind the tower. They've all been out of action since the ban. He died a year or so after it was put in place." She gathered up her map and slotted it into her satchel. "It leads all the way up the valley. If you were going there, you could try restarting the . . ."

"No, thank you," said Ester firmly. She swiped the map into her Gauntlet. "You've already told us more than enough. We'll get out of your hair now."

Lux, Fera and Brace looked at Ester as she spoke, but she ignored them. She swung open the door and stepped outside, forcing Lux to squint at the sudden brightness. Where was she going? Lux, Fera and Brace trudged after her.

"Aren't you chasing it?"

Ester was down on the gravel, scanning the tree-line. When she heard Cinda's question, she sniffed. "Normally people round here don't want us involved."

"I don't," said Cinda defensively. "I just thought now you're here . . ."

Ester sighed. "There aren't enough of us," she explained. "We'll go back to the Light Hunters HQ and bring others."

Cinda frowned. She turned to Lux. "It's Lux, isn't it?"

He stopped halfway down the stairs.

"Your grandpa," she said. "Is he the real reason you're here?"

A puzzled look twisted Lux's features. His grandpa? What was she talking about? "Sorry?"

"Because of your grandpa," she said. "Is that why you're here?"

Lux felt suddenly hot. "I'm . . ." he hesitated. "I'm not sure what you're talking about."

Cinda looked around. "Ben Dowd. He was here yesterday."

Lux frowned. Cinda had seemed so nice when she'd visited his grandpa's workshop. She'd even brought them a homemade cake when she'd collected her compass. He couldn't believe she'd lie about something like that.

"No," said Cinda angrily, stepping outside her shack. "It's true."

Her tone made Lux stop. "What do you mean, he was here?" He held out a hand for the others to be quiet.

"I mean," said Cinda slowly, glancing behind her at the valley, "he passed by here yesterday on his way to the lair."

· CHAPTER 51 ·

Lux stumbled backwards. It couldn't be true. His grandpa had barely left the house for months. It just couldn't be true.

"I'm sorry," he said, "he what?"

"He dropped in yesterday," said Cinda simply. "He was going up to the lair."

Ester's ears pricked up. She climbed the steps so she was level with Lux. "Ben Dowd?"

"I should know," said Cinda defiantly. "He's been fixing my compasses for years."

Lux sank to his knees. Was this real?

"Was he on his own?" pressed Ester. "Was there anyone with him?"

"No, he was alone."

"What did he say?" asked Lux.

"He only stayed for a little while. He used to visit my dad when I was a kid. I gave him some food and showed him the map."

Lux's breathing was shallow, his mouth dry. It didn't make sense. Why would his grandpa be in Kofi? How would he even get there?

"But . . . but . . . why?"

Cinda shrugged. Fera laid a reassuring hand on Lux's shoulder.

"Listen," said Cinda awkwardly, "I never wanted to get involved in any of this. I never meant to say anything out of turn." She stepped back to the doorway, tripping over a bucket and steadying herself. "Good luck with . . . whatever you decide." She fixed them with a last, lingering stare and disappeared.

The closing door woke Lux from his thoughts. "That's not real, is it?" He looked at Ester, anxious. "He can't have come up here."

"I don't know." Ester strode down the stairs, crossing the gravel until she was outside the watchtower. Lux shrugged Fera's hand off his shoulder.

"Ester!" he shouted. His legs were shaky.

She didn't respond. She walked back to the others. "We have to get back to Dawnstar," she ordered. "My father needs to be briefed." She scooped up her bag and slung it on her back.

"But . . ." Lux stumbled so he was in front of her, ". . . we can't."

"The mission," said Ester, calling up a map on her Gauntlet. "No, in fact, *our* mission," she said sharply, gesturing to her, Fera and Brace, "was to gather information and report back."

"But how long will it take?" asked Lux.

"You two," Ester said to Fera and Brace, "gather your things.

We're leaving in one minute."

A ball of rage pressed up against Lux's throat. He turned Ester to face him, but she shunted him away.

"Can we even use the teleporter?" he cried desperately.

"No," said Fera. "It's one way only. Takes a lot of energy. You have to be near Tesla's lab to use it."

"Then how will we get back?"

"We'll call for a skyship as per my dad's original plan," said Ester, adjusting her Gauntlet.

"How long will that take?" Lux's voice rose in volume. Ester didn't answer so he appealed to Fera.

"The rest of today."

Lux leapt up. "Today? We don't have a day! The Cerberus might attack any time!" He pointed back to town. "There are hundreds of people down there. Thousands! What are they going to do if we're not around? They can't fight a Monster. And what about my grandpa? If he's really up there, we've got to help him. He's ill!"

Ester stood still, unmoving.

"Well?"

"We need support," said Ester. "There isn't a squad in Dawnstar that can take on a Monster alone. Especially not this one."

"So, call for backup," said Lux.

"The Shells are broken."

Lux kicked at the dirt. "The other Hunters won't get here in time! It's Dowd. D-O-W-D. We're already at the first 'D.' You can bet it'll attack when we hit the next one. Deimos would have planned it that way!"

"That's precisely why we can't fight this thing alone," said Ester hotly. "We might, *might* be able to slow it down long enough for help to come, *if* you're as good a Healer as my father believes. If we work as a team and we get our plan right and none of about a hundred other things go wrong." She sank to a knee in front of Lux. "But not Deimos too, Lux. We can't take them both on alone."

Lux reared up. "We're not alone! My grandpa's up there!"

"Lux," said Ester softly, "he's ill . . ."

"Which is why we need to help him!"

Ester sighed heavily. "What do you two think?"

Fera levered herself to her feet. "I don't know much about Deimos or anything like that." She waved a dismissive hand. "But I hate a bully. And that man's a bully. If he's had a part in these Monsters attacks, we're going to have to take him on at some point. The sooner we do that, the better. I'm in."

Ester dipped her head in understanding. She appealed to Brace, who shrugged.

"You know me," he said gamely, "any chance for a fight." Brace conjured a Light-bow and sent a fiery arrow into a nearby tree.

Ester faced the valley behind the watchtower, a grim look on her face.

"He's alive," said Lux. "I know it."

"Well," said Ester, resigned to their fate, "I guess that means we'd better go and get him."

· CHAPTER 52 ·

Before they set off, Ester put in a call to Tesla and Maya at Dawnstar in the blind hope her Shell might be broadcasting even if it wasn't receiving. She told them what they were about to do and requested support.

"Fingers crossed," she said.

"Fingers crossed," echoed Lux.

They marched past the watchtower and made their way down a stone path into the forest. Lux had never been this far into the Kofi countryside. The tree cover was significantly thicker than near town, so that he had to duck to avoid being slapped by low-hanging branches. Brace conjured a Light-blade and hacked at the trees, the bark hissing and sizzling as he cut. Ester checked the map.

"According to this, the cable-car station should be another half a mile."

When Ester and Brace set off again, Fera tugged Lux's arm to hang back. "I'm glad you did that," she said quietly.

"Did what?"

"Changed her mind. We've been watching these beasts for too long. I don't care if everyone hates Light Hunters around here. People have been dying. They can turn their backs on us all they like, but that doesn't change our job. It's about time we got out there and actually fought these Monsters." She held out her hands, wisps of Light emanating from her fingertips. "You're not the only one with a reason to hate Cerberuses."

Lux walked on for a few paces, puzzled. What did she mean, he wasn't the only one? After a second, he asked.

"It's nothing," said Fera evasively. "I shouldn't have said anything."

"No, tell me."

"Honestly, it's nothing."

"Please."

Fera sighed in defeat. "Brace told you I was a Lindhelm Lancehart, didn't he?"

"Yes."

"Well . . . part of coming from a rich family, in my daddy's eyes at least, is the responsibility you have to your people. My daddy pays an entire village of people to work at his farm – literally an entire village. A Cerberus attacked us all when I was seven. I guess I've had a . . ." she paused, choosing her words carefully, "a kind of vendetta against them ever since."

"I bet you're glad Juno got this mission then," said Lux.

"Let's just say I'll be happy when there are no more of them left."

They walked on for a few paces. Fera nudged Lux in the ribs. "Ignore me," she said cheerfully. "I'm taking your mind off where it should be. Focus on your grandpa." She returned Lux's smile and skipped ahead to help Brace.

Lux walked on alone. He thought about what Fera had said. He'd been so focussed on protecting Kofi and Daven, and on ending the Cerberus, that it had never occurred to him that the others would all have their own reasons for being there. For being Light Hunters. Ester, with her mother beneath the crater. Fera, with the Cerberus back on her farm. Brace, with his uncle. Even Tesla and the Behemoth. It only made Lux even more determined to help the people of Kofi and Daven.

Soon, the trees thinned, revealing a winding stone path. Lux spied a dark shape ahead. He stiffened, worried it might be Deimos or his people. But it was too big. It had to be the cable-car station.

"I think we've got it."

The station was situated in a dip in the ground, surrounded by trees and bushes. It was a two-storey building, constructed of a dull, black metal and inlaid with glass panels. The place had been abandoned for a while, and most of the panes were cracked or smashed. Vines crawled up the walls, entering the building and warping the metal.

Lux approached the main entrance – blocked from the path by a thick, thorny bush. He searched for Brace, who winked and used his Light-blade to slice through. The burning smell reminded Lux of beach bonfires he and Maya used to have back in Daven.

"Makes you want a hot-dog," joked Brace.

"Are we sure this place is safe?" Lux asked Ester.

"It's as safe as it looks."

"No, I mean, Deimos."

Ester said nothing.

Lux sidestepped Brace, taking care not to catch his clothes on any sharp branches. He pulled at the door handle. It came away in his hand.

Inside, the station smelled earthy, just like a greenhouse. Lux kicked aside a few plants and made his way into the central chamber. The interior resembled the skybus station back in Daven. The far wall was open, with two thick wires shooting out into a batch of young trees. From there, they climbed into the valley. Two cars were parked in the station. Both had smashed windows and were splattered with rust.

It was Fera who found the station controls. The lower section was covered with knobs and dials, while the upper bore a single pull-switch. A cable ran from the panel over Lux's left shoulder. There, lifeless, stood the system's Light-engine.

Lux pointed it out to Ester, who motioned for Brace to carve a route through. Fera followed, forming a *Bolt* between her fingers.

"Not too much," Ester warned. "We don't want to overload it."

Fera expanded her *Bolt* until it was as big as her forearm, then thrust it forwards. It flew towards the engine and crashed into it, rocking the entire building and dislodging a shower of twigs and leaves. The *Bolt's* tendrils burrowed inside. A high-pitched wail sounded from the machine. The engine rumbled and the motor whirred into action. The two parked cars shuddered. Was that it? Had she got it going? Lux breathed a sigh of relief when the cables buzzed and began dragging the cars around.

"Nice one, kiddo," said Brace to Fera.

"I know we've got a job to do," said Ester, nodding at the smashed, rusted cabins approaching the station, "but it's probably best if we get there in one piece. Let's wait for a better one."

Lux tapped his foot, urging the cars to hurry. Outside, the arriving cars scraped at the low trees, leaving a perfectly straight edge at the top of the canopy. Soon, a pristine vehicle arrived.

"This is our ride," said Ester.

There was no obvious way to stop the machine while it was running, so Lux, Fera and Brace leapt into the moving cabin. Once Lux was inside, he turned to help Ester. She gave herself a run-up, then jumped, barrelling into his midriff and sending them both sprawling. Lux sagged in relief when he realised everyone was safely on board, even as his heart pounded. He burst out laughing, all the stress and tension of the last few hours spilling out of him in a great rush. Brace, Fera and Ester joined in.

"What now?" asked Lux, when they'd all calmed down.

"Now," said Ester grimly, "we hunt a Monster."

· CHAPTER 53 ·

The cable-car contained two padded benches. Lux selected one with Ester, while Fera and Brace chose the opposite. They all looked out the window as the car jerked up the valley. The station shrank until it disappeared, then the Monster watchtower and Cinda's shack. Further back, the land fell away, revealing a view like the one Lux had seen from the cliff-top. Only this time he could see further – past Daven's lighthouse and all the way out to sea.

When even this grew fuzzy in the late afternoon haze, Lux shifted so he could see ahead of them.

Somewhere out there was the Cerberus.

The cables threaded centrally up a wide, lush green valley. A thin stream zig-zagged down to Kofi's waterfalls, and crowning the vale was a snow-flecked mountain. Here and there were pockets of sheep, and Lux spied what seemed to be a pack of Monster spawn. He pointed them out to Ester.

"They'll only get thicker as we get closer to its lair," she said. "But if we end the big one, they die too. There's that, at least."

Lux took in the land. Just this tiny area had an entire Cerberus and its spawn to deal with. How many more towns across the world had a Monster stalking nearby? How many people went to bed scared every night, wondering if the next day would bring an attack? Lux clenched his jaw as he thought of Deimos, controlling Monsters, setting them loose. A man who'd once fought for good, fought to protect people. What had happened? How had he become so . . . evil?

"Shade," said Ester, staring up at the mountain. "It twists people."

Lux looked at her like she was a mind-reader.

"Lux, anyone could read your face." Ester put a hand on his forearm. "Look, just concentrate on your grandpa and the Cerberus for now. We'll go after the puppet-master later."

Lux stood up and stretched. For the first time since they'd eaten with Legau in the Howling Hydra, he felt like he could catch his breath. Over his shoulder, the sun burst out from behind a cloud, casting a soft, peach glow all over the land. Lux rolled his shoulders, happy to feel the warmth.

"Do we have a plan?" Brace asked Ester.

Lux listened for her answer, but none came.

"Shouldn't we use one of the set-ups we've been training?" pressed Brace.

"No good," said Ester. "Lux doesn't know them."

"So what *are* we going to do?" asked Lux curiously, realising he'd never healed anyone in an actual fight.

"We'll just have to wing it," said Ester. "Everyone play their role and adapt to whatever happens."

"What about grandpa?"

Ester looked up. "Lux, even if your grandpa *is* up there, he's ill. He's not going to be able to do much. We'll just have to keep him out of harm's way."

All of a sudden, there was a deafening boom in the valley. The cable-car lurched upwards, throwing them all to the floor. As it climbed, the glass cracked, spraying shards all over them. Lux scrambled to pick splinters out of his skin as the vehicle reached the apex of its swing and accelerated down again, dumping him and Ester on Fera and Brace. Wind rushed in through the exposed front, roaring and whistling.

Ester clambered over Brace, trying to stand. But every time the car bounced, she tumbled back down.

"What was that?" asked Lux desperately.

"Was it the wire?" said Fera.

Their questions were answered by a loud, terrifying roar – one so blood-curdling that Lux had to cover his ears to block it out. The car rocked again as an enormous shadowy shape appeared in the side window. Four massive, sharp claws narrowly missed Fera and Brace as they dived out of the way.

Lux staggered upright for a better look. He saw a creature so colossal – so terrifyingly, dizzyingly immense – that he gasped. It had to be as tall as Daven's watchtower, and as wide as a house. A rotten stench emanated from its grease-matted fur, and it hung from one tree-trunk arm off their car. Lux and the creature locked eyes and Lux saw a perfectly vertical scar – blackened and charred.

It was the Cerberus.

Lux was momentarily distracted by a shadow moving rapidly across the valley floor. The Monster's free arm hit the car, obliterating the sole remaining window. The creature clung to what was left, trying to reach the Hunters. High-pitched *pings* issued from the cable above. Ester caught Brace's eye. Brace nodded and conjured a Light-bow, firing an arrow into the Cerberus's flesh. Immediately, it bellowed and retracted its arm, rocking the car violently. Lux tumbled again, smashing into the metal with his temple and slamming his ankle on the ground.

Was it..? Who was..? Where..? Lux tried to think as he came out of a fog.

"What are we going to do?" he heard Fera stammer. "We can't fight in here. It'll rip us to pieces!"

Ester scanned their surroundings, then staggered upright and scrambled up the Cerberus's remaining paw to the top of the car. The creature swiped at her as she moved, but Brace slashed at its claw with a Light-blade, sending a piece thudding into Lux's chest.

"Get ready!" shouted Ester. She extended a Light-blade from her Gauntlet and thrust it up into the metal roof, tearing off a panel and tossing it out of the car. Lux lost sight of her as she pulled herself through. He heard footsteps above. Then Ester appeared again. "Hold onto something!"

Lux gripped his seat as Fera and Brace clutched theirs. All they could hear the Cerberus's heavy breathing. Then came a hissing near the roof. Sparks of Light flew into the air and there was a sharp ping. The car jerked wildly.

"*Oh wow,*" thought Lux dizzily, realising Ester's plan. *Surely she's not going to...? She can't...*

But before he could think anything else, there was a final, loud *shhviiip* and the cable gave way.

And then they were falling.

· CHAPTER 54 ·

Lux lay motionless, drifting in and out of consciousness. He was dimly aware of someone moaning nearby. He tried to open his eyes, but his lids were like iron weights. Had Ester really just dropped them from the sky?

When he finally woke, a familiar face hovered over him. "Grandpa!"

"Lux!" The old man smiled and gathered him up for a hug.

Lux ignored a flash of pain in his neck and hugged his grandpa, gripping him tight. "What are you doing up here?"

Lux's grandpa pulled away, looking at Lux. He was lying in what remained of the cable-car. The seat Lux had clung to during their descent had been torn clean away. Ester and Fera were beside him. An ugly red bruise had formed on Ester's leg, and Fera's arm was twisted awkwardly behind her back. Brace was wedged up against a dislodged seat. Seeing Lux, he forced a weak smile, revealing three missing teeth. He winced as his cheek muscles tugged at a cut under his left eye.

"Hey buddy," he croaked.

Lux's grandpa patted Lux to check he was all right. "When I heard about the deaths, I knew it was the Cerberus. I had to come. I had a feeling Nova would drop a team in to fight this thing." He winked mischievously at Brace. "I didn't think you'd *literally* drop in."

"Grandpa," said Lux, "you need to go home. You're ill."

The old man's eyes wandered to Ester, Fera and Brace. "I might be unwell, but I'd say I'm the healthiest one here right now."

"We can handle this," assured Lux.

"Young man," said his grandpa, "I've been tucked up at that workshop for too long." He shuffled over to Fera and Ester and checked them for injuries. "I am responsible for the damage this Cerberus has caused. People died because of my mistake and that same mistake also brought about Deimos's rise." Lux's grandpa looked up, his eyes blazing. "If I'm to die soon, I want to take this slobbering beast with me."

Lux frowned. "But . . ."

"Lux," snapped his grandpa, "I'm doing this whether you and Ester agree or not. Now, we need to get a move on. He'll be back soon."

"Who?" asked Lux impatiently, an image of Deimos suddenly appearing in his mind.

"The Cerberus," said Lux's grandpa, returning to the car's opening. "Are you all right to throw a few casts?"

Lux looked at his hands. *I barely feel okay to talk,* he thought. But when he spoke, he said, "I think so."

"That's my boy. Heal them up. Get them to their feet. I never liked throwing freshly healed Hunters straight back into action, but this time will have to be an exception." His grandpa wrinkled his nose. "I'm going to look around."

"Where are we?" asked Lux curiously. His grandpa ducked so Lux could see outside. There was a shallow pool about fifty metres in diameter, ringed by a granite wall. A waterfall similar to Kofi's flowed over this, except its water ran a translucent pink. Lux tracked the flow to its source, where he saw a pile of ravaged sheep carcases. "Ugh." He retched. "We're at its lair."

"Be quick," said Lux's grandpa. "I'll be back."

Lux started with Brace, who seemed like he'd recover quickest.

"Come on then," croaked Brace jokingly, forcing a smile as Lux clasped his hands, "let's see our wonderkid in action."

Lux grew a *Heal* and propelled it at Brace. The blue haze crawled over him like a spider's web, pulling torn flesh together and repairing damaged teeth, before coalescing by his chest and exploding in a flash of Light.

"Man, I forgot how *good* that feels," said Brace jubilantly. He touched his healed eye. "I wish *I* could do that."

"If you want me to do it next time you're injured," kidded Lux, "get out there and help my grandpa."

"No rest for the wicked, eh?" Brace crawled past Lux, keeping his head down so as not to bump it. "Wouldn't have it any other way."

He disappeared, singing a tune Lux had never heard about dropping a Monster into a pit of spikes.

Lux hobbled over to Fera and Ester and performed a similar ritual on them – healing their arms and legs respectively. It was amazing how much damage a Monster could do with just one blow.

Fera came to first, rubbing her arm. "What happened?"

"The Monster," said Lux simply.

"Oh yeah." Fera slumped.

"Where are we?" asked Ester, sitting up suddenly, her eyes panicked as if she'd just seen a ghost.

"We've landed at its lair." Lux pressed Ester down gently as she tried to get up. Really she should have had a day's rest, but a minute was better than nothing. "My grandpa's here."

Ester studied Lux. The moment was broken by a shout from outside. Lux's grandpa was moving around the pool, stopping every few paces to set a *Trap* cast. Brace followed, periodically *whooping* with excitement. Ester froze when she saw Lux's grandpa, her expression poised somewhere between happiness and incomprehension.

"So he is," she said to Lux. "Come on then, let's finish this."

· CHAPTER 55 ·

Lux's grandpa noticed Ester as soon as she exited the car. Their eyes met and a moment of understanding passed between them. Then Lux's grandpa returned to his casts. Ester helped him.

"Are you ready?" Fera asked Lux excitedly as they followed. She clapped her hands to generate sparks of Light.

Am I ready? Lux thought. *Ready to fight my first proper Monster?* "Not really," he said lamely.

"All you have to do with those magic hands of yours is fix us if we get hurt. That shouldn't be a problem for Light Hunter royalty now, should it?" Fera nudged his ribs playfully.

No sooner had her elbow connected than there was a deafening roar from the forest. All the Hunters stopped what they were doing and looked to Lux's grandpa. He nodded grimly.

Ester launched into action, ordering Fera and Brace to higher ground – Fera to a thin ridge by the waterfall, Brace on top of the tumbled cable-car.

"Stay up there as long as you can. Don't be drawn in unless you absolutely have to. If this thing backs us into a corner, we're done. The more range we have, the better."

Fera and Brace bounded through the water. When Brace arrived at the cable-car, he conjured a Light-bow and fired an arrow excitedly upwards. Ester scanned the clearing, choosing a place for herself.

"What about me?" said Lux anxiously. "Where am I supposed to go?"

"Sorry Lux," said Ester. "I keep forgetting you've not trained this stuff. Healers move. You've got to be moving constantly. If one of us gets hit, be there before we even feel it. Just, whatever you do, don't get caught."

Easier said than done, thought Lux gloomily.

Lux's grandpa waved for Lux to join him by the pool. Lux stepped from the grass verge into the cold water – shock numbing his toes – and splashed across. The old man squinted at the forest where they'd heard the roar.

"I guess Nova told you about my past," he said softly.

"Yes."

"It was important you didn't know." Lux's grandpa brought his hands to his chest and kindled Light as he'd done a thousand times back in his Daven workshop.

"I know," said Lux hoarsely. "I was angry at first, but I think I understand now."

His grandpa lifted a hand off his chest and ruffled Lux's hair. "You're the best Light manipulator I've ever seen," he said proudly. "You might not understand that yet, but it's true. Stick to what I've taught you and you'll be fine."

The Monster roared again, this time a lot closer. The sound rumbled around the clearing, echoing off the granite walls. The trees shuddered, shaking loose branches and leaves. Ester looked at each of the Hunters in turn.

"For Daven and Kofi."

Their eyes flashed. "For Daven and Kofi."

The Cerberus burst out of the forest, bounding into the shallow pool, its three heads writhing wildly, snorting and growling. The creature was even more terrifying up close than it had been from the cable-car. How could they possibly defeat it? Its teeth were as big as Lux's forearms and as sharp as knives. But it was the Cerberus's eyes that really captivated Lux – six fiery-red beads, glowing in the gloom.

The Monster thrashed in the pool and surveyed the clearing, twisting its heads. One froze, glaring at Ester. She held herself steady as its two other heads joined the first. The Cerberus watched to see what Ester would do, then it roared. It lifted its front legs, slammed them into the water and charged.

Instantly, arrows of Light shot past Lux as Brace – still perched on the cable-car – unleashed a barrage. Fera joined him, firing projectiles – *Bolts*, Lux guessed, although they might have been *Flames* for all he could see in the chaos. Suddenly, he felt cold and his skin goosepimpled. Nestled in his grandpa's chest was an

Ice cast. His grandpa let it fly and the jagged chunk of ice shot forward, thudding into the Cerberus's leg.

Despite the barrage, the Monster continued to gallop at Ester, who dipped her right shoulder, touching the ground. The Monster followed as simultaneously Ester sprang to her left, twisting so she was side-on and unleashing a Light-blade from her Gauntlet. She rammed it into the Monster's flesh. The Cerberus screeched in pain as its momentum carried it into the cliff-face. Ester landed by the pool, her Light-blade still drawn.

Lux stood with his mouth open. "Whoa!"

His grandpa slapped him on the back. "Focus!"

Lux followed his grandpa as he waded through the water, sending *Ice* after *Ice* at the Monster, pinning it to the wall. Fera joined him, tossing a mix of *Bolts* and *Flames*. From behind, Brace fired his bow – arrows flashing past with flickering Light.

Ester stood beside the Monster, watching it closely. The Cerberus thrashed about, pivoting under the cliff and shaking its heads violently.

"Break!" she yelled, throwing up a hand. Fera, Brace and Lux's grandpa stopped immediately and moved from their positions. It was all so tight and impressive to Lux. His grandpa waded back to the clearing's east side, Brace scrambled down from the cable-car and climbed into one of the trees, and Fera edged carefully along the ridge, until her back was just metres from the waterfall. Suddenly, Lux's legs turned to jelly. He was alone with the Monster in the pool. He stumbled over his own feet, tripping and splashing as he joined his grandpa.

· CHAPTER 56 ·

As Lux moved, he left ripples in the water. Ester, Fera and Brace watched agonisingly as they expanded towards the Monster's legs.

When they hit the Cerberus it froze, its gaze locked on Lux. It launched high in the air and landed, poised to attack. Lux let out an involuntary yelp and dragged his legs through the water as fast as he could – in and out, in and out. His grandpa and Fera threw casts at the Cerberus, trying to distract it. *More,* thought Lux, *more!*

Ester studied the situation and shook her head. "Brace!" she shouted.

Brace dismissed his Light-bow and replaced it with a Light-dagger. Lux looked around just in time to see him aim it at the Monster. The next thing he knew, Brace had vanished with a glittering Light flash. He re-materialised less than a second later near the Cerberus's left leg, his route marked by a fizzing blue trail.

"Whoa!" Brace said excitedly, throwing out his arms to steady himself. "I love doing that!"

The Monster heard Brace's voice and sent a head to investigate. It spotted him and let out a terrifying roar. As Lux finally reached his grandpa, Brace began to back away, dismissing his Light-dagger and wading through the pool towards the cliffs.

"Brace!" shouted Ester, leaping over an uprooted tree and sprinting towards the water. "You go one way and I'll go the other. Lead him over the *Traps*."

Brace continued through the pool, dropping spikes of Light. They solidified when they hit the lake, freezing everything around them. The Cerberus planted a paw on one and screeched in agony as the trap exploded in a shower of Light. Similar explosions popped across the pool as it crashed on. The Cerberus lashed out at Brace, flinging him towards the cable-car. Brace thudded into the metal and slumped to the ground.

Immediately, Lux grew a *Heal* as Ester veered to intercept the Monster. She tapped her Gauntlet, prompting small Light clumps to appear. She tossed one at the Cerberus's heads, where it exploded in a red-hot fireball.

Ester's attack enraged the Monster, which emitted such a high-pitched scream that Lux had to finish his *Heal* early and thrust his hands to his ears. The Light arced across the pool and crashed over Brace like a wave. Had it caught him right? Lux couldn't see. Ester passed the Monster, one boot on the verge. Fera conjured a static *Bolt* – a golden spear – and tossed it down ahead of Ester, who gathered it up and hurled it like a javelin. The *Bolt* sliced through the clearing, slamming into one of the Cerberus's heads. Its momentum carried it through, out the other side and into another of the creature's necks, where it lodged in leathery skin.

Good shot, thought Lux.

"Now!" roared Ester.

The Hunters moved as a pack, throwing wave after wave of Light. The Monster shuddered as the energy rammed into its skin. Then its rear legs buckled, and suddenly it was kneeling, half submerged. The Hunters circled, throwing so many casts that Lux could barely see. Brace staggered to his feet after Lux's *Heal.* He leapt like a grasshopper when he saw he was missing an attack and charged at the Monster, conjuring his Light-bow.

The Cerberus sank so it was almost on the bottom of the pool. Ester raised a fist for them to stop. Their final casts slammed into the Monster's skin and fizzled out. Ester stalked the creature, her Light-blade poised. Lux heard the Cerberus's laboured breathing – rasping, scratchy breaths that didn't quite fill its lungs – and saw dozens of scorch-marks where their Light had connected. Ester's eyes found Lux's grandpa. He nodded. At his signal, Ester raised her blade, ready to drop.

But she froze.

A look of fear twisted her face.

What had she spotted? Seeing Ester afraid frightened Lux, and he fought an urge to jump behind his grandpa. Instead, he bunched his fists and tried to stop himself shaking. In the water, Ester pumped her legs, trying to get away.

"Get down!" she yelled desperately.

Lux dropped instantly. His grandpa sank to his knees too. On the other side, Fera and Brace backed out of the water and flung themselves down. Lux wanted to ask his grandpa what was happening, but before he could the Cerberus swung its two remaining heads towards him. Where before Lux had seen four small, beady eyes, he now saw four pulsing red globes, the same red as Deimos's Shade. The globes expanded rapidly, so that they were as big as Lux's head, then Lux himself. There was a terrible, metallic grinding sound, building in pitch, louder and louder, until Lux felt physically sick.

Then they exploded.

· CHAPTER 57 ·

The violent force flung Lux and the others back. Lux glimpsed Ester, who was heading for a set of jagged rocks near the waterfall, and threw a quick *Catch*. The cast unfolded with an electric clash, covering the entire cave opening. Ester careened into it – the Light swallowing her completely, before pulsing once and spitting her to the ground. She lay motionless, water lapping at her feet.

Lux, Fera and Brace writhed and rolled on the ground, trying to breathe. Between them, the Cerberus reared angrily, water pouring off its back. Lux's grandpa was still down. Lux stumbled over.

"Lux!" Fera called from across the clearing. "Ester!"

Lux glanced at their squad leader, who hadn't moved. "I know!" he shouted. "Just keep it busy."

Lux heard the familiar crackle of Brace's Light-bow and

repeated *whumps* as Fera rained *Bolts* and *Flames* on the Monster. Lux stooped by his grandpa and helped him up. But he shoved Lux away.

"Save her," he said fiercely, pointing at Ester.

Lux looked between them. It couldn't be one or the other, he had to heal them both. His grandpa waved him away again.

"Go!"

Lux's route to Ester was blocked by the Monster and a storm of swirling Light. How could he possibly make it across without being seen?

Lux approached the Cerberus's back leg. He was tempted to lash out but managed to control himself. Instead, a vicious *Bolt* from Fera pierced its thigh. The Monster lurched in pain. A shadow flashed past Lux as one of its legs appeared directly above him. Lux dived aside, landing head-first in the water as the limb smashed down. Slowly, he staggered to his feet.

He was close to Ester now, who was still flat on her back. Her face was pale, and she was barely breathing. Lux kindled a *Heal*, craning his neck to see what was happening behind him.

"Lux!" shouted Brace desperately. "Hurry!"

"I am hurrying!"

Lux channelled energy into the cast. Soon, it began to vibrate and he let it go. The Light broke over Ester. Lux dived behind a rock and raised his arms, ready to throw a *Protect* barrier should the Cerberus turn in their direction. But Brace was still dancing with his bow, keeping the Monster busy. Lux stared at the scene – a thundering, cataclysmic storm of Light – and shook his head. It wasn't working. He'd been wrong. They couldn't beat a Cerberus with only five of them. They'd never been able to. He'd risked all their lives for nothing.

Ester rubbed her neck as she woke up. "What happened?"

"I don't know," Lux said vaguely, shaking himself back to the present. "Its eyes went red and there was an explosion."

"I saw that," snapped Ester impatiently. "Where's the spawn?"

"What do you mean?"

Ester stared at Lux, waiting for an answer. Then she lost her patience and scanned the clearing. A wave of resignation washed over her. Lined up around the top of the cliff, pacing and snarling, was an army of Monster spawn.

"Where did they come from?" asked Lux.

"The explosion." Ester tapped her Gauntlet. "It was Shade. A call. It's called all Monster spawn in the area. We're overrun. We have to finish this now."

A spire of Light shot up from Ester's Gauntlet, whistling into the air and exploding like a firework. Lux picked out a shape – a cross, tilted diagonally. Fera and Brace saw it too. They recognised the symbol and backed out of the water.

"What's going on?" asked Lux, puzzled.

"Go to your grandpa," said Ester firmly. She went to the cliff by the waterfall and started to climb. "Tell him '*Bolt.*' All right?"

"Okay, but . . ."

"Lux! Go!"

Lux jumped. He skirted the pool, heading for his grandpa, who'd crawled back to the cable-car, still injured. Lux skipped as one of Fera's *Flames* landed just behind him. The cast exploded, leaving a patch of burning ground. Brace continued to dance around the Monster, trying to lead it away.

"Please hurry!" he shouted to Fera, leaping to avoid the Cerberus's tail.

"I am!" yelled Fera irritably, as another *Flame* exploded close to Lux. She gritted her teeth. "Lux, get out of my way!"

Lux pumped his legs, jumping over bushes and boulders and tree roots. The *Flames* followed him, tracing a circle around the pool.

"Fera . . ." pleaded Brace.

"Nearly done!"

Lux reached the cable-car just as Fera's wall of flames swept in front of him and continued on around the pool, the heat burning his cheeks. His grandpa was leaning on the car, still fighting to breathe. His face was pale, and he had a cut on his forehead which trailed blood down his cheek.

"Are you all right?" asked Lux.

"I'm fine," said his grandpa weakly. "Where's Ester?"

Lux turned to where he'd last seen her. He spotted her pulling herself over the cliff-edge. As she staggered to her feet, all the Monster spawn nearby froze, their ears pricked and spikes tensed. They bellowed angrily, beating their chests. Ester drew a Light-blade from her Gauntlet as they closed in.

Lux's grandpa pulled a face. "That damn girl."

"She wanted me to give you a message," said Lux. Above them, Ester dived into the spawn, swinging her blade.

Lux's grandpa waited.

"*Bolt.*"

"So, it's all or nothing," said his grandpa tonelessly. He looked up at Ester. "So be it." He stumbled towards Fera's ring of fire. "You'd better stand back for this bit," he warned Lux. Lux backed up towards the cliff. He heard a gurgling, throaty snarl as one of the Monsters – a two-legged, spiny, fish-like creature – slithered over the cliff-edge and started to climb down towards him.

"Um ..."

"Not now," said his grandpa.

Fera hurled a last *Flame*, closing her ring of fire. Brace slipped through the gap just in time, before turning and baiting the Monster again. In the pool, the Cerberus spun wildly, snorting steam.

Lux glanced anxiously at the Monster descending the cliff, liquid oozing from its mouth. More followed. Further along, Ester was slicing through the spawn. Lux willed her to see him and help. Instead, she froze midway through a killing strike and stared down at Fera's flaming wall. She skipped to an overhang. "Brace!"

He looked up.

"Now!"

Brace altered direction, passing beneath Ester. The Cerberus followed. When it reached the cliff, Brace collapsed behind Fera's ring of fire. The Monster pulled up at his sudden disappearance and probed the fire, cautiously extending a head and jerking it back whenever it touched a flame. Directly above, Ester gripped her Light-blade tightly, breathed once and leapt from the cliff, swinging the blade down as she fell. She landed on the Cerberus's back, ramming the sword into its flesh. The Cerberus reared in pain. Ester unhooked her Gauntlt from her wrist, so that it hung from the Light-blade, still embedded in the Monster's back, and used her momentum to somersaut backwards, slamming into the cliff-face.

As the Monster crumpled under Ester's blade, Fera and Lux's grandpa hurled a flurry of *Bolts* into the water. The casts swirled to an electrical storm – a galaxy of blue and white and gold sparks that whipped the Cerberus. The creature shuddered and roared.

"It's working!" shouted Lux exctedly.

Brace was back on his feet now and he scrambled to a platform over the fire wall. His view was blocked by clouds of smoke, but he fired arrows all the same, punching holes in the grey.

Lux checked on the Monster spawn on the cliff-face. They were no longer descending. *It's working,* he thought, *it's really working!*

Slowly, the Cerberus sank in the pool, flinching as sparks shot up and burned its skin. Lux's grandpa paused and faced Lux. His eyes were sad. He smiled warmly, his voice so soft it was almost a whisper.

"See you, buddy."

With that, he turned back to the Monster, raised both hands and unleashed such an almighty *Bolt* that it threw him back into the cable-car, cracking his head. The *Bolt* ploughed into the water like a bomb, exploding in a hot, white flash. It shot a wave of sparks into the clearing that expanded horizontally, crashing into the cliff behind Lux. He dived towards his grandpa and covered his head with his hands. What had he done?

The white flash receded. Fera and Brace shared a relieved

glance, studying the lifeless Cerberus in the pool. Fera threw a *Flood* at the fire, dampening it so Brace could step through. He reached the first of the Cerberus's heads and nudged it with his boot. He hopped back, looking for signs of life.

But there were none.

They had done the impossible.

The Monster and its spawn were dead.

· CHAPTER 58 ·

But so, too, was Lux's grandpa.

When Lux saw the old man's head hit the cable-car, he scrambled over. His grandpa's eyes were shut and his normally-ruddy cheeks were pale. Lux wedged his shoulder into his grandpa's armpit and lifted him so he was leaning against the cable-car. His head lolled onto his chest.

"Come! Quick!" he shouted desperately. "He's hurt!"

The others raced over. Ester knelt while Fera and Brace hung back. She loosened Lux's grandpa's shirt.

"Heal!" she ordered him. "Heal!"

Lux struggled to breathe. He was so tired that just the thought of throwing another cast made him want to collapse. But he brought his hands to his chest and formed a *Heal* between his fingertips.

He guided it carefully so it was over his grandpa and let go. The Light drifted to his grandpa's forehead, ballooning to encompass his body. Ester pressed her ear to Lux's grandpa's mouth, but Lux could already see there was nothing. He formed another *Heal*, this one more powerful, and floated it to his grandpa. The energy pulsed around him and disappeared.

"No!" groaned Lux. "No! No! No!" He sank down, tears streaming from his eyes. He banged the ground with his fist, cutting his skin. Behind him, Fera and Brace exchanged a worried glance.

Lux had come so far. He'd overcome so much. And for what? To see his grandpa die? To see the person who'd looked after him, taught him all he knew about Light, go the same way as his parents and sister? That couldn't be how it ended. Lux sat up, as tense as a rock. There had to be something he could do. He was a Healer. One by one, he went through all the casts his grandpa had taught him – *Heal, Protect, Catch*. Or perhaps a combination? Maybe a *Heal* and a *Protect* together . . .

Lux's stomach gave a jolt. "*Revive!*"

Ester looked across. Brace leapt up. "Yes!" he said excitedly. "That'll work."

"Wait," said Fera, "wasn't there a time-limit?"

"Four minutes and forty-six seconds," said Lux quickly.

"It hasn't been that long," said Brace, clapping his back. "Do it!"

Ester was kneeling by Lux's grandpa. Lux looked across at her. She nodded. Lux leapt to his feet. He adopted a position over his grandpa, closed his eyes and travelled back to Tesla's laboratory.

He'd only seen the *Revive* book once, but he could visualise the cast. He progressed through it in his mind, building it between his fingers, holding it steady. His heart thudded. He had one chance.

Behind him, Fera and Brace stared. Brace's fingers were crossed.

Lux channelled Light until he'd imbued the cast with everything he had left. He positioned it over his grandpa, where it hovered momentarily before descending. But it stopped before making contact. Lux peered at the Light, feeling hot and panicky. Had he made a mistake?

"Come on," cried Fera desperately.

"I can't," snapped Lux. "It won't let me."

Suddenly, the clearing flooded with crimson energy, casting blood-red shadows over the grass. There was a tearing sound, like the world itself was ripping apart. Instinctively, all the Hunters looked up. Hanging in the sky, as if some invisible fabric had peeled away to reveal what was really underneath, was an enormous skyship. Several smaller ships flashed into existence close-by. Lux looked again at the flagship – a monolithic black craft with entire sections torn away and enough battle scars for a lifetime. On deck, a small crew ranged back and forth. One figure stood out – a stocky man with a pock-marked face, bulky black overcoat and wide-brimmed hat.

"Oh no," said Lux despondently, "that's Deimos!"

· CHAPTER 59 ·

Fera and Brace leapt into attack stance. Brace conjured a Light-bow and drew an arrow. But before they could cast anything a red, mist-like energy surrounded them – solidifying and shrinking until they were each enclosed in a bubble of Shade. Lux and Ester came next – Ester still on the ground, her shins trapped so she could barely move. Lux hammered at his field with his fists, his right-hand lancing with pain where he'd cut it. He had to get out of there. In their bubbles, Fera and Brace were throwing all they had at the energy – *Bolts, Flames,* arrows. Nothing dented them.

"What is this?" yelled Fera.

"You know what it is," said Ester, glancing frustratedly at her Gauntlet, still embedded in the Cerberus's back. "It's Shade. Stop attacking it. You'll only hurt yourselves."

As if to prove this, Fera threw a final, frustrated flurry of *Flames*, only for a spark to bounce off the Shade and lodge in her shirt. She patted at the fire, extinguishing it as quickly as she could. Then she held her breath, squinting through wisps of smoke, suddenly aware she was in an inescapable bubble.

Deimos's skyship had descended now so it was surrounded by the clearing, its serpent figurehead splitting the waterfall. Other skyships hovered above, their engines flashing red. Lux looked at his grandpa, the *Revive* cast still hovering precariously nearby. His cheeks were ashen in the skyship's shadow.

A metal gangplank extended out of the ship, ratcheting down to the ground. Deimos appeared at the top, two of his crew flanking him. He raised a hand, instructing them to remain. He descended the gangplank slowly, taking in the clearing. He reached the verge and circled the water, heading for the cable-car.

"Let me out!" shouted Lux when Deimos was within earshot, kicking at his Shade barrier.

"Lux," said Deimos, his voice as cold and hard as steel, "explain to me how doing that would contribute to my plans."

"Let. Me. Out!"

"I'm afraid not." Deimos paused at Lux's bubble. He extended a finger, pressing at the haze. "I was initially going to do this the nice way." He took a handkerchief out of his pocket and wiped his finger. "But your . . ." He paused, grasping for the right word, ". . . actions have forced us down a different route."

Deimos approached Ester's bubble and stooped so his face was close to hers. He smirked mockingly and then spun away, his coat flowing behind him. "There was a time I'd have been here with you, fighting this thing." He gestured at the Cerberus. "Did you know that Lux? I gave all I had to the Light Hunters. We saved so *many*. I lost many friends. And what did I receive in return?" He struck a severed wire hanging from the cable-car. "Nothing! No, less than nothing!"

Lux glanced at his grandpa and the *Revive*. In his mind, he tried to keep count of the time.

"After the attack on Daven . . ." A black cloud darkened Deimos's face as he uttered the word. ". . . I learned a way to stop the Monster attacks for good. But the fools at Dawnstar wouldn't listen."

"Shade is evil," said Lux hoarsely.

Deimos scoffed. "And how would you know? Because Artello Nova told you? Shade is not evil, Lux. Shade is a force more powerful even than Light." Deimos paced to the cable car and back. "The ruins that litter these lands once belonged to our ancestors, did you know that? Thousands of years ago. Their understanding of Light and Shade far exceeded our own."

Lux glanced at his grandpa again. The *Revive* pulsed. He was running out of time.

"It was the Ancients who created the Monsters, gave them life, shaped and controlled them. If we could harness their understanding, find out what they knew. We could use Shade to stop these attacks once and for all."

"But you're *using* Monsters to attack towns!" cried Ester.

Deimos turned to her. "A necessary sacrifice. My research

points to an ark – a structure used by the Ancients to contain all their knowledge on Light and Shade. It is believed to be buried beneath a town in this region. But your leaders wouldn't let me search for it, so I have taken matters into my own hands."

"You're killing innocent people!" said Lux. "Look at you, look at what you've become."

Deimos tilted his head. "Innocent?" He sneered. "The people of Daven and Kofi turned their backs on those who tried to help them."

"Their only fault is to wish for a world without Light," said Ester. "You'd give them a nightmare full of Shade."

For a moment, there was silence. Lux looked again at his grandpa. "Deimos," he pleaded, "let me go."

Lux's words woke Deimos from a daydream. "Yes," he said distantly, approaching Lux's bubble, "yes. If your powers are as great as your grandpa and Nova believe, then I might at last have found what I require to unlock the Ancients' secrets."

Deimos sank to a knee in front of Lux's grandpa and studied his face. With his free hand, he flicked Lux's *Revive* cast aside. It drifted slowly to the ground, where it dissipated in the early evening air. Lux slumped to his knees. He felt like he'd been stabbed in the heart.

"Ben Dowd," said Deimos admiringly. "I learned a lot from this man. There was Shade to him, even if he didn't know it."

"There was not!" yelled Lux.

Deimos regarded Lux, surprised at his emotion. "But I have surpassed even him now. In time, all the people of this world will see my methods. They will turn from Light as Kofi and Daven have. Light is no match for Shade. You, too, will realise that soon, Lux."

"No!" Lux bared his teeth. "I'm a Light Hunter."

"A Light Hunter?" Deimos's eyebrows knitted together. "You, of all people should know how worthless they really are.

"But no matter," he said abruptly, turning to his ship. "As I said before, if you refuse to join me by choice, I will take you by force." Lux's bubble rose, dumping him onto his back. The others, still locked in their cages, hammered at their Shade.

But not Lux.

Something was happening inside him. Images flashed before him – the first time his grandpa had shown him how to cast Light, his first day at school, his grandpa waving goodbye at the gate, the time they went hiking and got caught in a thunderstorm so loud Lux thought the world was ending, the day Lux's grandpa informed him he was dying. These images churned in Lux – rolling and tumbling and reeling – each carrying with it an emotion that sliced at his insides. Somewhere, Lux felt a power start to form – small at first, like a tiny spark of Light. But it grew and grew, until he could feel it pressing at him – something new, a sensation he'd never felt before. In his bubble, Lux glowed a translucent, shimmering purple. The sensation prickled his skin. A low hum made Deimos look around. Lux met his eyes for the briefest of moments.

Then he blew.

· CHAPTER 60 ·

"About flipping time."

Lux heard the words from a long way away, like he was underwater. He tried to open his eyes, but they felt as heavy as iron.

"He always does this. Every time he sleeps over at the orphanage, he pretends he's still asleep so he can have a few more minutes snoozing."

Lux opened his eyes. He was lying on a hospital bed in a cool, breezy room, with Maya and Brace staring down at him.

"Hey!" said Brace happily.

"Huggghh," attempted Lux, but his words came out as a slur.

"Is he actually awake this time?" Lux recognised Fera's excited voice.

"He's . . ." Brace frowned, not quite sure how to put it, "well, he sounds a bit like a Monster with toothache, but I think he's awake."

Lux tried to sit up, but Fera appeared at his side and guided him back down. "No no no," she said gently, "not yet, Lux. You've been out of it for a long time. You need to rest."

Lux noticed Fera was hobbling. "What happened?" he asked. "Where am I?"

"You're at Dawnstar. In the healing wing. And don't you worry about what happened. We can deal with that later." Fera turned to Maya and Brace. "Keep him in bed. Don't let him get up. I'm going to get Ester."

Fera limped back to her seat, scooped up the book she'd been reading and headed out of the room, leaving Lux alone with Maya and Brace.

"I can't believe you're awake!" Maya said excitedly. "You've been asleep for two weeks."

"Two . . ." Lux echoed weakly. Had he really been asleep that long?

"We've been waiting for you. You really did a number on yourself. *And* these guys." Maya nodded at Brace, who lifted his bandaged right arm.

"You sprained my wrist. And you broke Fera's leg. In two places!"

"Don't be sill . . ."

Lux stopped. It all came back to him in a great, flowing rush. Kofi. Cinda. The Monster's lair. The Cerberus. Deimos. Purple. His explosion. "I . . . I . . ."

"Ah, don't worry about it," said Brace cheerfully. "What's a life-threatening injury or two among squad-mates?"

"I . . . exploded," said Lux. It sounded weird to say it. "I remember."

"Yes," confirmed Brace, "I knew there was something strange about you the first time I met you. I didn't know you'd spontaneously explode though. Came as a bit of a surprise, if I'm honest."

Lux laughed, but it tugged at a cut underneath his lip. "Ow."

"Probably best not to laugh," advised Maya.

There was the sound of hurrying footsteps in the corridor. Fera and Ester appeared in the doorway. Ester rushed to Lux's bed and took his hand.

"You're back. We've all been so worried."

"I'm so sorry," said Lux. "I don't know what happened . . ."

"Lux, we know you didn't mean any of it, so you can stop apologising right now. I'm just glad we're all here to talk about it."

An image of Lux's grandpa flashed into his mind. Ester must have read this on his face, because she turned to Maya, Fera and Brace. "Can you give me a few minutes with Lux, please?"

Maya and Brace seemed reluctant to leave, lingering by his bed. But at Ester's insistent stare they gathered up their things and trudged outside.

"Your grandpa?" said Ester, when they were gone.

"Yes."

Ester shook her head sadly. "I'm sorry, Lux."

Lux felt a huge weight fall on him, so that he could hardly breathe. A tear formed in his eye, but he bit his lip hard to stop it falling.

"It was nothing you did," added Ester quickly. "He'd already passed from the Monster. Your . . . thing came after."

Ester explained everything that had happened. Or, at least, the things Tesla had worked out. How Lux's explosion had been heard for miles, blanketing the countryside in the violet haze. How it destroyed every tree in a two-mile radius and triggered an enormous shelf of mud and rock to roll down the valley. How, when it had all finally ended, the terrified townspeople had hiked the flattened ground to the clearing and found it empty – a Dawnstar ship having just picked up the Hunters. And how the only evidence they found of a battle taking place was a black ring burned into the rocks at about the height of a twelve-year-old boy.

Ester told him how in the following weeks, successive squads of Hunters had scoured the Kofi countryside, collecting every scrap of damaged skyship for delivery to Tesla's laboratory. How they'd found little, and that the few pieces they did find were mangled by Lux's explosion.

And she told him of Fera's broken leg and Brace's wrist. How Ester herself had survived almost entirely unscathed. How Maya and Fera and Brace had sat by Lux's bed for two weeks, whispering jokes into his ears and telling him stories, waiting for him to wake up.

"What was it, Ester?" asked Lux quietly, when she'd finished her tale. "What did I do?"

"Don't worry about that for now. Just focus on recovering. Y were in a bit of trouble there, the Healers tell me."

Lux didn't like the sound of that. But he wasn't going to

on it. His grandpa never complained about being unwell and neither would he.

"What?" said Ester, looking sideways at Lux as she caught a knowing smile on his face.

"We did it."

"Did what?"

"*It*," said Lux. He winced as the word tugged his cut. "We beat a Monster with just one squad."

"Is that your way of trying to tell me you were right and I was wrong, Lux Dowd?"

"No . . ."

"Because you were right and I was wrong." Ester inclined her head, cautioning Lux that this would be the only time she'd admit to such a thing. Then she pecked him on the forehead. "Get better, kiddo."

Maya, Fera and Brace were already at the door as Ester got up to leave. Ester grabbed Fera and Brace as she passed. "Unfortunately, you two are needed in the training hall for the next hour."

Brace stiffened. "But we trained this morning . . ."

He was cut off by Fera, who elbowed him in the ribs. She and Ester fixed him with such a meaningful stare that even Lux, still waking up, understood Ester was trying to give him some time 'lone with Maya.

"Oooh," said Brace, finally catching on. "I see." He darted 's bed, made two finger guns and popped off a couple of o'hots at Lux. "We'll be back in a bit pal. Need to debrief ."

"Yes," said Fera, limping over and leaving her book as a present on Lux's bedside table, "we'll catch you in a bit. Don't do too much, all right?"

They left the room, leaving Lux alone with Maya. During Lux and Ester's conversation, Maya had dashed to Dawnstar's kitchen and snagged a bag of toffees from the cook there. She tore it open and laid it on Lux's bed.

"Thought these might cheer you up. I know you're meant to bring grapes, but well . . . who wants grapes?"

Lux popped a toffee into his mouth. It was the first thing he'd eaten in two weeks and it tasted amazing. "Thanks."

"You really worried me there, you know?" Maya perched on his bed. "I really thought you weren't going to wake up, and then I don't know who I'd have done missions with. Brace is fun, but he's not quite as sharp as you."

Lux felt his heart swell just a bit.

"I'm sorry about your granddad," added Maya. "Ester told me. It's really sad. He was always nice to me. Even if he did make me sweep the workshop sometimes."

Lux wanted to say something but found that the words jumbled in his mouth. It was still too raw.

"Can you believe all this started with that Monster spawn back in Daven harbour? My leg. Seems like ages ago, doesn't it?"

"Yeah," said Lux.

There was a moment's silence.

"Why did it have to happen, Maya? Grandpa?"

"Oh, I don't know Lux." Maya frowned, frustrated. She wanted to say something more helpful. "Mrs Piper always used to say that the sun sets and rises when it's ready. I used to think she was talking about the actual sun, but after all this, I'm not sure."

Lux opened another toffee and chucked one to Maya.

"I know one thing though," she said, lobbing the sweet up and catching it in her mouth, "your grandpa would be proud of what you all achieved. The Cerberus. *Our* Cerberus. Gone."

Maya was right. For a decade, Daven had dealt with the aftermath of its last Monster attack. It had taken Lux's mum and dad, his sister, and Maya's parents too, as well as countless others. But now the Cerberus was gone. It would never come back. His grandpa would have been proud.

But it had cost them all so, so much.

Lux said none of this to Maya. Instead, they sat together in the cool afternoon sun, popping toffees into their mouths and seeing who could finish first.

· CHAPTER 61 ·

It took Lux longer to recover than the others, who'd been somewhat protected from his blast by Deimos's Shade bubbles. Lux stayed in hospital for weeks, undergoing healing sessions with Dawnstar's best Healers and trying to patch up his own body with everything he'd learned. He was visited by Artello Nova and Tesla, who listened intently as Lux tried to explain what had happened in the clearing – the storm of emotion, the shattering explosion. But truthfully, Lux didn't know what had happened. He just knew he never wanted it to happen again.

Out in the world, things carried on as normal. Sightings of Monsters poured into Dawnstar – some urgent, some less so. Nova fielded each personally, as he always had, searching for any patterns that might be connected to Deimos. He found nothing, although many nights saw him up past midnight, gazing into his fire and trying to work it all out. Why they'd failed to find a single molecule of Shade on any of the skyship scraps they'd recovered, nor any bodies in the flattened countryside. That Deimos's skyship was known to be infused with the dark energy was a worry he kept from Lux.

Nor did they find any evidence of Lux's grandpa, despite a long search. In the end, it was decided to hold a funeral without the body, on the crater floor where he was said to have walked happily during his years at Dawnstar. Lux watched on proudly as a procession of Hunters, both old and new, took to a podium erected at the crater's centre, each praising the man he'd known as grandpa.

And then it was over.

Life went back to normal. Or, as close to normal as it ever could. Lux did his best to keep going – waking up, scoffing breakfast with Fera and Brace, training with them and Ester during the morning, disappearing off to the skyship hangar in the afternoon to watch Brace start his pilot training, visiting Tesla in his laboratory or sitting at Dawnstar's back entrance with Fera as she told him funny stories about their instructors, and how Tesla was all wrong when he said Flame casts were not the best way to cook toast.

To Lux's surprise, Tesla himself made a personal request of Nova that Maya be allowed to stay on at Dawnstar as his apprentice, even going so far as to personally write a letter to Mrs Piper at Maya's orphanage. Though he never actually told her in as many words, Lux felt better having Maya around. And all the other Hunters felt better now Tesla had someone to keep him on his toes.

Back in Squad Juno's dorm, a new picture appeared on Brace's wall – an ugly Cerberus with a big black cross through the middle. A matching sketch appeared on Fera's wall.

"I thought you didn't put Monster pictures up," Brace said to her, as he attached a new Cerberus badge to his uniform, showing Lux where to place his.

"I don't," said Fera. A knowing look passed between her and Lux. "This one's just different, that's all."

It came to pass that yet another series of Monster attacks had been reported – a Fire-Drake terrorising the residents of Ringtown. Nova had gone easy on Squad Juno in the months after Lux's incident. But with the Fire-Drake, he considered it time to put them back in the field. He summoned them to his room at the top of Dawnstar. After explaining their mission, he ordered everyone but Lux to leave. He led him through the red door to the balcony.

Lux found him leaning on the balustrade, staring up at the sky. "She is high tonight," said Nova, indicating a twinkling, yellow-gold star hanging high in the darkness.

"Who is?"

"Juno. The star your squad is named after."

Lux peered up at the sky. He'd never seen Juno before. It was beautiful – pin sharp and sparkling.

"I am going to be honest," Nova informed Lux, "I do not know whether you got him."

"Deimos?"

"We never found a body, nor sign of his ship." Nova shifted his injured arm. "He may still be out there."

"Do you think he's behind the Fire-Drake?"

"He could be." Nova put a reassuring hand on Lux's shoulder. "Listen, we understand if you are not ready to go out yet."

Lux nudged the balcony with his boot.

"How do you feel about it? You know you will always have a home here. We owe your grandpa that. But there are plenty of jobs less dangerous at Dawnstar, certainly less dangerous than being a Light Hunter."

Lux looked up. "I'm scared."

"You are safe here, Lux."

"Not that," said Lux, his face twisting with frustration. "I'm scared of me, of what I did. What if it happens again?"

Nova leaned on the balcony rail, gazing down at the cherry blossoms in the courtyard. "Lux, I do not know what occurred back in that clearing. You did something no-one at Dawnstar has ever encountered, something powerful. Maybe even dangerous. But your grandpa believed in you, believed you were good. You hurt nobody that day that did not deserve it. Remember that."

"But what if I do it again?"

"Then we will make sure you do not hurt anyone."

Lux was still hesitant.

"Listen, it is a big, bad world out there, and it is filled with dangerous Monsters. You have proven yourself on the battlefield, and more importantly you are part of a squad now. Squad Juno. They need you. You are their Healer. Come on, what do you say?"

Lux stared at cherry blossoms, swaying in the breeze. He recalled similar blossoms outside the memorial garden in Daven where the victims of the Cerberus attack – his sister and parents included – were laid to rest. He thought of his grandpa – the greatest Luminary the Light Hunters had ever known. A man who'd sacrificed his life to destroy the Cerberus. A man who'd encouraged Lux to nurture his talent, trust in Light despite what everyone else around him said. He thought of Kofi, and Ringtown, and a dozen other places across the region, all cowering under the spectre of Monsters. Finally, he thought of Maya, Ester, Fera and Brace, about all they'd been through, his new family. He couldn't let them down. Any of them.

Lux walked back into Nova's room and turned to the old man, a ball of Light between his fingers. The Light reflected off his face, casting a soft blue glow. Lux fixed Nova with a determined stare, his decision made.

"Let's go hunt some Monsters!"

SQUAD JUNO

The Monsters of the Light Hunters' world are big, bad and dangerous. Because of this, a Light Hunter never faces a Monster alone. Lux's squad, Squad Juno, contains Hunters from four different classes – Tech, Healer, Conjuror and Archer – all of whom wear special badges to signify their class, as well as any Monsters they've defeated. Find out more below . . .

TECH: The Jack of All Trades. Techs can't manipulate Light personally, but they wear a special Gauntlet device to let them interact with the energy. *Traps*, *Shields*, maps and Light-blades. You name it, a Tech can do it!

HEALER: Healers channel the force of Light to help their injured squad-mates. *Heal*, *Protect* and *Revive* are just some of the tools in a Healer's handbook. If you find a Monster's bitten off your toe, it's a Healer you need!

CONJUROR: Conjurors are queens and kings of destruction. The Light Hunters' damage-dealers – they wouldn't be caught dead without their fiery *Flames*, freezing *Ices* and crackling *Bolts*. Little tip: stand well back!

ARCHER: Archers are masters of stealth. Zipping around the battlefield unnoticed, leaving only a glittering trail of Light in their wake, it's rare to see an Archer without their trusty Light-bow and dagger, as well as a handful of *Traps*.

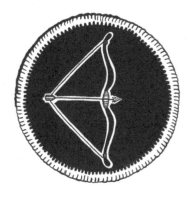

CERBERUS: What good would a Light Hunter be without a Monster? And what Monster is scarier than a Cerberus? An enormous, three-headed, slavering dog, with razor-sharp teeth, foot-long claws and a roar as loud as an earthquake. You wouldn't want to meet one on a dark night!

ACKNOWLEDGEMENTS

Creating a book is a bit like keeping an iceberg afloat. The author stands on the bit poking above the water, waving their hands triumphantly, but really there's a whole bunch of people kicking their legs beneath the surface, turning those little black squiggly sentences into a beautiful finished product.

With that in mind, a few thanks ...

First, the team at UCLAN – Hazel, Debbie, Becky. You showed faith in my story and for that I will be forever grateful. Here's hoping there are many more tales in the Light Hunters world.

Thanks also to Chris for his sculptor's scalpel – much appreciated. I learned a lot. Thanks also to George Ermos for his stunning artwork. Love it.

Lauren at Bell Lomax Moreton. It's fair to say you have to

be patient working with me, and you're the most patient person out there. Thanks for the honesty, hard work and great ideas.

The wonderful people at Brilliant Book Award, Reading Rampage, RED award, Salford Book Award and Derbyshire School's Book Award – you all know who you are . . . thank you. There's a whole army of people supporting the children's writing scene, and these people are the vanguard.

Thanks to Joanne Rowling and Philip Pullman and any one of a dozen other authors who inspire me to do this whole thing. Write more books so I can read them!

To my mum, who's put up with me for 36 years. Salut!

To my beautiful and patient wife, who listens to me yabber on about my latest creative trials and tribulations every night before we go to sleep – you're an inspiration and a rock at the same time.

And of course, thanks to all the little people who read these stories. It's a bit of a cliché to say at this point, but it's your enthusiasm, excitement and enjoyment that make the whole writing process worthwhile. Hope you got lost in this tale of Light Hunters and Monsters.

Bon appetit!
Dan Walker

ASK THE AUTHOR

Do you recognize yourself in Lux? A little bit, in that he's curious about the world and wants to help others. But mostly I just wanted him to have 'drive.' I wanted Lux to be propelling his own story, taking action even if no-one else was. I hope I achieved that.

If you were a Light Hunter, would you be a Healer, Conjuror, Archer or Tech? I would definitely be a Healer. Conjurors have to throw so much Light that I'm sure it would hurt their fingertips after a while. Archers are constantly whizzing around, so I'd probably get dizzy. And as a Tech everyone would be constantly asking you to get your map out. I think Healer gets to do the cool, life-saving stuff without the hassle!

This world is so complex, how long did it take to think of all the intricate details? I can't speak for other authors, but while I plan out my worlds in a fair amount of detail as I outline the plot, characters, etc. I also find a lot of ideas coming to me as I write. Little thoughts pop into my head and I decide whether they fit the world or not. So, it's a long process, but divided into little chunks.

What were your favourite books when you were Lux's age? I loved a series of books called the *Hardy Boys*. They featured two young lads – amateur detectives – who'd go around solving mysteries. I also read a lot of Enid Blyton. And I think when I was around Lux's age *Jurassic Park*, Stephen Spielberg's movie, came out. I remember being fascinated by the Michael Crichton book it was based on and reading it over and over.

As a child, what scared you the most? I had a children's story book and inside it was a picture of three trees, with horrible, grotesque, gnarled faces. One night, I was going to sleep and noticed that my brown curtains, when bunched together, looked exactly like those trees. I found it hard to sleep for a very long time after that . . .

Did you take inspiration from other fictional creatures when creating your own monsters? Most of the Monsters mentioned in the book are monsters from the mythologies of our world – Cerberus, drake, etc. But I think for future books I might well make up my own. A dog-bird with human-sized claws and so many eyes that you can't hide from it, anyone?

Why did you pick the Cerberus as the main Monster in the book? I've always really liked the idea of Cerberuses – enormous, house-sized, snarling, vicious, multi-headed dogs from Greek mythology. Nicknamed the 'Hellhound of Hades.' Dog of Hell. Seemed appropriate as the Monster to be attacking Lux's hometown.

Were you inspired by any fantasy novels when writing the book? Enormously so. And games, and movies. I love fantasy as a genre and am always reading and watching examples of it. Fairy tales and epic poems also had an influence on *The Light Hunters*, with their enormous creatures and diverse casts of heroes.

What kind of research did you do before starting the novel? Did you take any inspiration from the physics of light and colour or did you create the Light Hunters' universe from scratch? Light in my book is very different to the light in our world, so I didn't do any research as such. I tend to like making up the more fantastical elements of my books, as this allows you to be more creative than if you tie yourself to our world. The key is to make sure that the details of your world are consistent.

What was the most difficult part to depict throughout the book? Characters are always the hardest part of a book to get right. When it comes to descriptive passages, I tend to just close my eyes and write down what I see. But you want readers to *care* about your characters' journeys. For this to be the case, they have to ring true. And to get them to ring true you have to develop their journeys carefully and at a believable pace. This takes work but is worth it when you get it right.

How important do you think strong female characters are to the story? Absolutely enormously so. I'd go as far to say if there aren't strong female characters in your story, then as a writer you're just not reflecting our world accurately. I also grew up in a house full of women, so if I didn't have strong characters I think I'd get verbally beaten to a pulp!

Was Elon Musk your inspiration for Tesla's name? No, Tesla was loosely inspired by an old inventor from the 19th century called Nikola Tesla. He basically did a lot of work making electricity – as we know it – possible.

Is the ability of being a Light Hunter genetic? Or can it be developed? It's not genetic in the sense that people don't have a gene 'for' Light. But it is innate. You're either able to manipulate Light or you're not. Techs use devices called Gauntlets to manipulate Light, but they can't actually wield it.

Will we find out more about Lux's parents and sister in later books? Probably not (although I'd never say never.) One of the things about the Light Hunters' world is that the Monsters are constantly attacking towns and cities. People are in danger almost every day. Some even lose their lives – this is what makes the Light Hunters so important. Lux's family are just like everyone else. They're not special. They were in the wrong place at the wrong time. But the motivation their death gave Lux was supremely important.

Why aren't the Light Hunters respected like Lux respects them? I don't want to give too much away, as this is quite an important part of the story, but I can say that something happened in the past that led to people being unsure about Light and how safe it is. Lux doesn't feel like this because he has first-hand experience of Light.

IF YOU LIKE THIS, YOU'LL LOVE ...

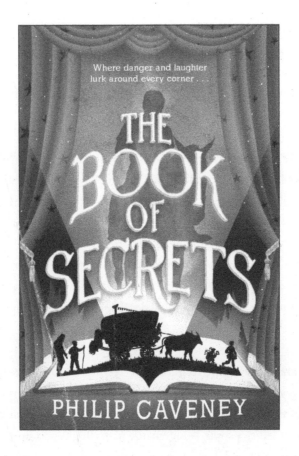

Where danger and laughter lurk around every corner . . .

THE BOOK OF SECRETS

PHILIP CAVENEY

COMING APRIL 2020!

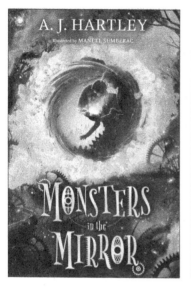

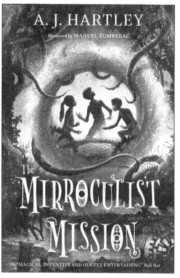

FOR MORE
INFORMATION VISIT:

www.uclanpublishing.com

HAVE YOU EVER WONDERED
HOW BOOKS ARE MADE?

UCLan Publishing are based in the North of England and involve BA Publishing and MA Publishing students from the University of Central Lancashire at every stage of the publishing process.

BA Publishing and MA Publishing students are based within our company and work on producing books as part of their course – some of which are selected to be published and printed by UCLan Publishing. Students also gain first-hand experience of negotiating with buyers, conceiving and running innovative high-level events to leverage sales, as well as running content creation business enterprises.

Our approach to business and teaching has been recognised academically and within the publishing industry. We have been awarded Best Newcomer at the Independent Publishing Guild Awards (2019) and a *Times* Higher Education Award for Excellence and Innovation in the Arts(2018).

As our business continues to grow, so too does the experience our students have upon entering UCLan Publishing.

To find out more, please visit
www.uclanpublishing.com/courses/